Death at St. Asprey's School

In this new Carolus Deene story, set in a boys' prep. school, it is very much a case of blackmail amongst the blackboards, of mayhem and murder, where Carolus is called in to investigate a series of spooky happenings at St. Asprey's. But the ghostly charades are only a prelude to murder, and a fight to the death for Carolus.

Written tautly, and with delightful understanding of schoolboy love and language—and the ennui of the teachers in the suffocatingly tense atmosphere of the school—this is an exciting detective story.

T0165670

Death at
St. Asprey's School

LEO BRUCE

Academy Chicago

An imprint of Chicago Review Press
814 North Franklin Street
Chicago, Illinois 60610

Printed and bound in the U.S.A. Second
printing, 1987

Library of Congress Cataloging in Publication Data

Bruce, Leo, 1903–1980.
    Death at St. Asprey's School.

    Reprint. Originally published: London: W.H. Allen, 1967.
    I.   Title.
PR6005.R673D39   1984   823'.912   84-388
ISBN 978-0-89733-094-7 (pbk.)

Death at St. Asprey's School

Chapter One

On an airless June night the boys in a dormitory of St. Asprey's Preparatory School were disturbed when one of them, a certain Maitland, had a violent fit of hysterics. Normally a dull if not lethargic boy, he seemed now to have entirely lost control of himself as he shrieked and pointed to the window.

One of the boys immediately ran for Matron, and a skinny woman with prominent teeth appeared, wrapped in a workmanlike dressing-gown. Slapping Maitland sharply across the face she reduced him to gloomy but less hysterical tears and the remaining boys to silence.

"Whatever's the matter with you?" she asked the snuffling Maitland, the son of a prominent ecclesiastic.

"I saw something," said Maitland desperately.

Curiosity, a constant and lively emotion in Matron, came to the fore. There had been so many ugly and frightening events at the school lately that she was prepared for almost any revelation.

"Well, what?" she asked impatiently.

"A f . . . face," blubbered Maitland.

This had implications for Matron.

"Where?" she asked.

"At the window."

The dormitory was on the first floor. Matron began to hope that the boy was suffering from delusions.

"What kind of face?"

"A man's."

"Someone you knew?"

Maitland shook his head.

"It was a beastly sort of face," he said.

"It's gone now," Matron pointed out. "You'd all better get to sleep or I shall have to call Mr. Sconer."

Just as she reached the door, Maitland shouted wildly—
"Don't turn the lights out, Matron!"

Even the bravest warrior may realize when the odds against him are too high and Matron saw that the situation had gone beyond her authority.

"Whatever's the matter with you?" she asked, but she left the lights on while she went to call for help.

This came in the person of the headmaster's wife, a formidable woman named Muriel Sconer who, through some association of ideas among the boys, was known as Mrs. Bun. Unlike Matron who had rushed to the dormitory at the first summons, Mrs. Bun had given some moments to her appearance and approached in a magnificent *peignoir*.

"What's the matter, Matron?" she asked with lofty confidence in her own ability to deal coolly with any crisis.

"It's Maitland, Mrs. Sconer," Matron said. "He's been having a nightmare, I think. I found him quite hysterical, saying he saw a face at the window."

"Nonsense," said Mrs. Sconer sharply.

"He does not want the light out," Matron exclaimed.

"Now, boys," called Mrs. Sconer in her rich contralto voice, "you must all go to sleep and stop all this silliness. I'm surprised at you, Maitland. I thought you were more sensible."

"Please, Mrs. Sconer, I *did* see it."

"Another word from you and you'll Go To The Study tomorrow," said Mrs. Sconer peremptorily. This produced silence, as might be anticipated, but not acquiescence in the extinguishing of lights.

"*Please* don't turn the light out, Mrs. Sconer." cried Maitland desperately.

"You'd better go to Matron's room and get a pill," was Mrs. Sconer's lofty rejoinder. "Give him an aspirin," she whispered to Matron. "You must have been dreaming. Now off to sleep, the lot of you."

Returning to her room, however, Mrs. Sconer was far less calm than she appeared. The events of that term were enough to disturb anyone, even this monumental woman who dominated her world so arrogantly. Only a week ago there had been a scare in the Senior Dormitory when all the boys, serious youngsters of twelve and thirteen years, swore to having seen what they variously called the Monk, the Old Friar or the Abbot. Their accounts of this phenomenon tallied and could not be shaken even under the threat of Mr. Sconer's cane. A 'man in grey like you saw in books' bearded, pale and tonsured, had passed through the dormitory 'mumbling Latin'. A ghost? Oddly enough they did not think it was a ghost. It seemed more real. A joke? No, they said, they were sure it wasn't a joke. It remained a mystery, but what seemed certain to the adults was that someone was deliberately disturbing the life of the school with these manifestations.

But such phenomena, unpleasant as they were and productive of anxious letters from parents, were not the worst influences over the once placid life of the school. Something hostile and corruptive was at work and everyone's nerves were on end. Tempers in the common-room were frayed and there had been a number of senseless outbreaks over trivialities. The happy and jocular relationships which had once been noticeable amongst the staff, when even Matron had been known to smile cautiously at the latest classroom anecdote, had turned to suspicion and secretiveness and Matron herself, so long believed to be a mere 'sneak', a laughable bearer of news to Mrs. Sconer, had become an almost satanic figure, a centre of malignant intrigue. Everywhere was tension, anxiety, distrust as though some tragic event was impending.

The actual events which were held responsible for this might not in themselves be thought world-shaking, but they seemed to have some occult significance to the overwrought nerves of the proprietors and staff of St. Asprey's. Footsteps had been heard in the passages at night, not the patter of boys' feet, but the measured pacing of a man, yet those who had been rash enough to open their doors had seen nobody. Lights, spoken of as 'lanterns' had been seen moving about the grounds when all Christian folk should have been sleeping.

When six Angora rabbits belonging to a boy called Charlesworth had been found one morning dead in their hutch, their skulls battered, it had aroused furious indignation and much sympathy for the owner, but no explanation for the crime had been found. The boys began to talk of Dracula and other creatures found in horror comics, and a stern censorship had to be exercised over Sunday letters. 'Dear Mother and Father, Last night we saw a gost' was no matter for laughter in a school which depended on parents' satisfaction with the education and living conditions for which they were paying high fees, and 'Dear Mother and Father, On Friday all Charlesworth's rabbits were slain by a Vampire', had to be erased and a new sheet of notepaper issued to the correspondent.

At long secret conferences Mr. and Mrs. Sconer, the proprietors of the school, discussed these matters, realizing their seriousness.

"What will happen on Sports Day I daren't think," said Mrs. Sconer. "The parents will hear the most grossly exaggerated stories. I shouldn't be surprised if we lose a dozen boys. You really must *do* something, Cosmo."

Her husband was a gaunt muscular man, rather ineffectual she had always thought, and usually respectful of her wishes.

"I don't see what is to be done," he said. "I've forbidden all pets after this term. We can't have them sending the creatures home now. In many cases the parents would not know how to feed them and would be most indignant at receiving a litter of guinea-pigs."

"Then get rid of Sime," said Mrs. Sconer.

Colin Sime was one of the assistant masters, a clever teacher according to Mr. Sconer and among the boys 'the most popular master in the school', but disliked by the staff and detested by Mrs. Sconer.

"I don't see how I can do that, my dear," said Mr. Sconer miserably. "Unless we have evidence that he is somehow involved in all this."

"Of course he is!" said Mrs. Sconer. "Anyone can see it. I've always told you that he's shifty and undesirable."

"But he's an excellent teacher. He gets the boys through the Common Entrance exam."

"There won't be any boys to be got through it very soon if things go on like this. That young man you've just taken on. . ."

11

"Mayring?"

"Yes. He was disgracefully rude to Matron yesterday. You will please tell him, Cosmo. Matron is quite irreplaceable, as I've told you before."

"She's not popular with the Men," said Mr. Sconer.

He was not voicing a wide generalization. 'The Men' were the assistant masters.

"I should think not. She's far too loyal to me for that. But I won't have that overdressed youth insulting her."

"Mayring is a first-rate cricket coach, my dear, and Parker is getting past it."

"Parker!" snapped Mrs. Sconer contemptuously. 'Jumbo' Parker was that faithful old assistant who had been at the school for twenty years and had no other home or interest— a type common to almost all English preparatory schools. Sconer said nothing when his wife brought out his name in that tone, though it was known that he depended on Parker in many ways. "The only man you've got who is at all worth his salary is Jim Stanley."

"He's not much of a disciplinarian," Sconer pointed out, making a notable under-statement.

"But he's a gentleman, which is more than you can say for the rest of them," his wife told him triumphantly. "As for Sime. . ."

Somewhat feebly Mr. Sconer pleaded urgent work. He did not want his wife's opinion on Sime, which he knew too well, to be repeated.

But in the days following the incident of 'the face at the window', the staff of St. Asprey's School, till then merely startled and worried by curious happenings, began to realize that there was something more sinister at work than a nocturnal practical joker and felt the first real pangs of fear. Once loosed in a small, fairly isolated community like this.

fear could grow and turn to terror, and this is what happened.

Its first serious manifestation came on the very next morning and was generally connected with that apparition. Young Arthur Mayring, who last term had been still at his public school, Radley or was it Uppingham? had obtained the headmaster's permission to bring back to the school a fox terrier puppy named Spike which he kept in the stables. The little creature was well-behaved and though Matron had blamed it for the presence of a flea in Stewart II's underpants, no one had ever had cause to complain that Spike was noisy or a nuisance.

Young Mayring had gone as usual to the stable after breakfast and found that his pet's throat had been cut and the puppy was lying dead in a pool of blood. A more experienced Man would have kept knowledge of this from the Boys, but Mayring was so badly shaken by his discovery, so furiously angry and so heartbroken that he confided in the first persons he met who happened to be Richardson and Plumber, two twelve-year-olds. Before morning school began there was not a pupil at St. Asprey's unaware that Mr. Mayring's dog had been foully murdered, and gory details ran from mouth-to-mouth.

It was the pool of blood that seemed to appeal to the common imagination and Mrs. Sconer lost her head a little when she heard of it.

"It's ruin," she said to her husband. "With Sports Day next week."

Not the Hartnell dress in which she had invested for the occasion, not all her crocodile charm with the parents would pacify their anxieties when they heard from their sons of the blood lust and horror abroad in the school. "You should never have engaged Mayring and certainly never allowed him to import livestock."

"My dear, I was scarcely to know. . ."

"I have warned you, Cosmo. Perhaps now you will give Sime notice."

"But what has Sime to do with this?"

"That is for you to find out. I am convinced he is in some way responsible."

"It seems to me like the work of a maniac."

"It is. And how do you know that it is not that of a homicidal one?"

"My dear . . . a dog. . ."

"The species is no proof. Next time it may be far worse."

"Really, Muriel. You speak as though we had to anticipate murder in the school."

"I should not be in the least surprised. Perhaps then you will realize that my advice should have been taken months ago."

"But *murder*. . ."

"It's no use your repeating the word, Cosmo. Matron believes her tea was tampered with the other day. She has her suspicions that someone it trying to poison her."

Mr. Sconer may inwardly have been crying 'good luck to him!' but his face continued to be sad and anxious.

"She must surely be exaggerating," he said. 'Matron says' was not his favourite phrase when it was spoken by his wife.

"She is a shrewd and competent person. I am thankful to have someone I can rely on in the school."

In the common-room that day not much was said, though at first there was sympathy for Mayring. His threats, however, of what he would do to his dog's assassin if he found him grew tiresome as the day went on and received no encouragement from the other Men who remained sullen and taut, resolving to lock their doors that night.

Richard Duckmore, the fourth of the five assistant

masters, who was always a highly-strung individual, showed signs of overstrain. His hands were unsteady and the twitch which always afflicted him grew more noticeable.

Two nights later the school was again aroused by piercing screams, this time from Matron herself. Mrs. Sconer hurried to her room and found her ally gibbering with disgust and horror as she pointed to her turned-back bed on which a dead rat was incongruously lying.

"I put my foot on it!" she yelled, her eyes staring wildly at the headmaster's wife.

"Some idiotic joke," suggested Mrs. Sconer.

"Joke! You call that a joke? I shall never be able to get into bed again. I could feel the fur!" went on Matron hysterically.

"Most unpleasant. Whoever did this shall be punished—I promise you that. If it is one of the Men he shall be dismissed instantly."

Matron had not yet pulled a dressing-gown over her sensible night gown and Mrs. Sconer could not help noticing that without reinforcement Matron's hair was inadequate to conceal her incipient baldness.

"I could not possibly sleep here," Matron warned her.

"The thing must be removed," said Mrs. Sconer majestically. "Wait—I'll call Parker."

In a few moments 'Jumbo' Parker, looking somewhat puffy and crimson, had picked up the corpse with a newspaper and carried it away. When a senior boy named Chavanne appeared from his dormitory Mrs. Sconer, forgetful for the first time that the boy's father was a millionaire with three younger sons to educate, spoke sharply.

"Back to bed this instant," she said.

"Please, Mrs. Sconer, I heard someone screaming."

"You heard nothing of the sort. Chavanne, unless you want to Go To The Study tomorrow."

15

Chavanne knew the emptiness of this threat.

"I thought the Vampire had struck again," he said.

"Don't be ridiculous. Matron was not feeling well. Now back you go to bed and don't talk a lot of nonsense to the other boys." Chavanne departed wondering and Mrs. Sconer continued to Matron—"You see what happens?"

Matron felt this was an implied reproach.

"I shall have to leave," she said. "I can't stand any more of this sort of thing."

"We'll talk about that in the morning," said Mrs. Sconer, sounding friendlier, as she prepared to return to her room.

The habit of years impelled Matron, even in this crisis, to confide her latest discovery.

"Jim Stanley and the Westerly girl went out together again this afternoon," she said.

'The Westerly girl' was Mollie Westerly, teacher of the most junior class, a pretty young person believed to be an heiress who had joined the staff that term.

"They did?"

"I saw them leave. Then Sime was up on the church tower again with the field glasses from the rifle range."

"You are sure?"

"Positive. I know he's watching them."

"It's all very disturbing, Matron. You had better sleep in the little spare room for tonight."

"Yes," said Matron. "I don't think I could sleep here again."

This was less positive than Matron's last refusal, but still argued her position. She had never liked her bedroom, and was determined to change it. Mrs. Sconer, however, had no intention of permitting the change.

"I don't wonder," she said with a benign smile. "It must have been horrid for you. We shall have to see that this room gets a good old turn-out tomorrow and a change of sheets and blankets."

"I don't know whether. . ."

"*Good* night, Matron," said Mrs. Sconer and with a speed remarkable in a woman so statuesque was gone.

She found her husband anxious and irritable.

"What wash that infernal noish?" he asked thickly for he had not put in his teeth.

"It was Matron," said Mrs. Sconer.

"Matron? What on earth wash matter with the woman?"

"Hysterics," said Mrs. Sconer concisely. "She's all right now."

"Shterish? There wash surely no need to make all that noish?"

"Don't be unimaginative, Cosmo. Someone had put a dead rat in her bed. Its enough to give anyone hysterics. I had to get Parker to remove it. They carry the most frightful germs, I believe."

"Bubonic plague," said Mr. Sconer knowingly. "Who put the thing in Matronsh bed?"

"What on earth's the use of asking such an absurd question, Cosmo? Do you think I should be standing here quietly if I knew? I have a pretty good idea, but that's another matter."

"You're going to say it-sh Shime I sherpposhe? Where do you think Shime could have got a dead rat from? And why would he put it in Matronsh bed? Itsh not loshical."

"Oh go to sleep, Cosmo. It's really no good talking to you. You'll let the school be ruined before you act."

Chapter Two

For some days there was no incident large enough to threaten the routine of St. Asprey's, though several members of the staff looked as though they were sleeping badly, and Horlick, the gardener, complained that his beds were trampled by large feet during the hours of darkness. Then happened something which could no longer be dismissed, by even the most sceptical, as sick humour at work, or as anything less than a serious, nearly fatal attack on one of the staff which some did not hesitate to call attempted murder.

The original building of St. Asprey's had been the manor house of Pyedown-Abdale, a village in Gloucestershire, for St. Asprey's, like every other preparatory school was situated in one of the healthiest positions in Great Britain. It was a very large house patched and added to at different periods and set among great whispering trees. Its nearest building was the church, a rather splendid piece of architecture which recalled by its size that Pyedown-Abdale, now a straggle of labourers' cottages, had once held an important wool market. The Rectory was on the village side of the church, so that the school buildings with a cottage or two were isolated from human habitation and watched over by the church tower. If Matron's story of Colin Sime was true, this fact had aided him in his observations, for she claimed that he climbed the tower with field glasses.

The boys attended eleven o'clock service on Sunday mornings and there was close co-operation between church and school, the Rector, the Reverend Austin Spancock, giving weekly divinity classes at the school, and Jumbo Parker having been for more than half of his twenty years at St. Asprey's organist and choirmaster at the church. A few terms earlier his tenure of this office had been threatened by Duckmore who was a far better organist but by dint of his years of past work he managed to retain it. A number of the boys, by special permission of their parents, democratically sang in the choir and attended choir practice.

Jumbo Parker, a stout and happy-faced man, enjoyed playing the organ almost as much as he enjoyed sitting in the bar of the Windmill Inn over a pint glass of rough cider. He did not play very well but was lucky in his instrument for the last squire of Pyedown-Abdale, whose heirs had sold the manor house cheaply to Mr. Sconer, had endowed the village church with an unusually fine organ. Jumbo occasionally walked across the fields to the church to play for his own entertainment, and almost invariably practised on Saturday afternoons. It was on the occasion of one of these Saturday visits that the Thing happened which destroyed the last vestiges of peace at St. Asprey's.

Jumbo had to tell the story so often afterwards that it fell into a series of clichés. He went, he said, intending to spend an hour at the organ. On that Saturday afternoon there happened to be an Away match and young Mayring had gone by coach with the team to play St. Bensons, another Cotswold school. Mr. and Mrs. Sconer were receiving a visit from some prospective parents. Several of the staff and a married couple named Ferris, whose son was at the school had gathered on a lawn behind the staff bungalow to practise archery, for it was a craze among the adults that term. These were Jim Stanley the third assistant, a man named Kneller, and Mollie Westerly. Duckmore, the other assistant, was in charge of the boys on the cricket field. So Jumbo Parker was free to indulge in one of his favourite occupations—playing the church organ.

He told how he strolled across the meadows delighting in the sunlight and without the smallest foreboding of anything unpleasant. He entered the church and it seemed its usual self, the faint musky smell and the light coming through the stained glass windows just as he had known them so well all these years. At first there was silence then he was aware of a faint moaning which seemed to come from the West end of the church.

Jumbo Parker described it afterwards as a somewhat eerie sound. His mind which had been easy during his walk, returned to the disturbing events of the last few weeks. He made his way towards the sound and realized that it came from beyond the oak door leading to the stairway to the tower. He opened this and to his alarm and horror released a human body which rolled to his feet. It was that of Colin Sime who was now unconscious.

Parker acted quickly. He gathered at once that Sime had fallen down the staircase from the loft above in which the bell-ringers performed. He saw that he was not dead but gravely injured. He made him as comfortable as he could with his head on a hassock then rushed out to get assistance. 'By the grace of God', as he said afterwards, he found the Rector arriving in his old car. (Mr. Spancock explained afterwards that he had seen someone on the tower of his church and as this had happened several times lately he had hurried across to investigate.)

The Rector was an elderly man with chin and forehead which both receded from the central and most prominent feature of his face, the tip of a large, almost triangular nose. He spoke in a throaty and hollow voice which lent itself to mimicry by choirboys and clipped his sentences to a minimum.

He took in the situation at a glance, or enough of it to tell him how to act.

"Stay here," he said to Parker in the curt way he normally adopted. "I'll get help."

Nothing more was said as the Rector drove hurriedly away. There were malicious suggestions afterwards that he might have gone to a nearby farm for the age-old expedient of a hurdle on which to carry the injured man, but that he preferred to make use of the members of his First Aid class who had to be gathered together in the village. The Rector was a keen believer in First Aid and this was his first chance to test the proficiency of his pupils. It was in fact more than half-an-hour before Sime had been placed, by the method prescribed in the book of instructions. on a stretcher. Only then was it realized that no one had phoned for a doctor or an ambulance. In these circumstances, the church being some distance from a telephone, it was decided to carry Sime across to the school and from there summon Dr. Cromarty. If it was necessary for Sime to go into hospital he could be moved from St. Asprey's.

The first words that Sime was heard to speak were brief and to the point.

"I was pushed," he said.

The doctor examined him and decided that the injury to his legs should be X-rayed for which he must be taken to hospital. But Sime resisted this passionately. He wanted to stay where he was, in his own room at the school, and nothing would induce him to enter a hospital. He appeared to have recovered at least from the shock and after much dispute, in which Dr. Cromarty told him tartly what kind of a fool he was, he got his own way and was left in bed, impotent to move but able to speak his mind.

The police were informed of the accident and of Sime's exclamation—"I was pushed." A cool and tactful Detective Sergeant named Haggard came to the school in a non-commital motorcar and saw Sime alone in his room on the very day of the accident, but this discretion did not prevent the story of Sime's having been the victim of violence from reaching the boys and had it not been for the strictest censorship that Sunday's letters would have begun: 'Dear Father and Mother, Yesterday someone shuvved Mr. Sime down the stairs of the church tower in an a tempt to murder him.'

At Mrs. Sconer's urgent behest, her husband implored Sime 'for the good of the school' not to tell everyone that there had been a deliberate attempt to injure him, but Sime rejected this and when Detective Sergeant Haggard was with him gave a full account of the matter.

"I felt it distinctly," he said. "Just as I reached the head of the long spiral staircase down from the bell-ringers' loft to the ground someone gave me a violent push and I lost my foothold. I feel I'm lucky to be alive."

Colin Sime was a hefty man, so hefty that all his clothes looked a little too small for him and one felt their seams might burst open to release the swollen flesh. His small eyes had the cunning of a pig's eyes and his whole presence suggested a vulgar, grasping and untrustworthy personality. Yet this was 'the most popular master in the school'.

Haggard may have wondered as others had done at the curious trends of small boys' hero-worship but he showed no sign of hostility.

"You were about to come down, Mr. Sime?"

"Yes."

"May I ask what had taken you to the church tower that afternoon?"

The question seemed quite unexpected.

"That has nothing to do with it," said Sime sharply. "Someone tried to murder me."

"Nevertheless I should like to get a complete picture. You must have had some reason for climbing the church tower."

"Architecture," said Sime impatiently.

"I see. Is the church tower here an interesting example of some period?"

"It has some gargoyles on it," said Sime, fortunately remembering a fact he had been told.

"And you wished to make a study of them?"

"That's it."

"Had you ever been up there before?"

"May have. Once or twice. What's that got to do with it?"

"A pair of field glasses was picked up at the foot of the stairs."

"Was it?"

"Were you carrying field glasses, Mr. Sime?"

"I daresay I was. Lovely view from the tower."

"You did not have them in order to make any particular observation?"

"No. No. The view."

"And the gargoyles. I see. You didn't suspect anyone's presence in the tower that afternoon?"

"Certainly not. Do you think I'm a fool? Whoever it was must have been hiding when I got there."

"Or perhaps followed you in?"

"Can't say. All I can tell you is I felt a violent shove and found myself falling down the stairs. Very unpleasant sensation. The next I knew was the Rector and Jumbo Parker staring down at me like a couple of owls."

"I see. You perhaps know that you have been seen going to the tower on previous occasions, Mr. Sime? There seems to have been some resentment about it. People supposed you were watching them."

"Ridiculous," said Sime.

"You know how people feel about that sort of thing. Is there anyone you suspect of wanting to injure you?"

"Injure? Whoever pushed me was trying to kill me. It's only by a miracle that I'm alive."

"Well, to kill you?"

"I daresay a lot of people would. This school's a hotbed of jealousy."

"Anyone in particular?"

"That's for you to find out. *I* don't know who it was shoved me down those steps. That's all I can say."

The Detective Sergeant after making a few more routine enquiries from Sime sought the headmaster and obtained certain details of everyone's movements that afternoon. Then, with a few pages of his notebook filled, he returned to his headquarters at Woldham. It may be safely guessed that in his report he conjectured fairly confidently that Sime did in fact know, or suspect, the identity of his assailant. If he had been quite in the dark about it, he would surely have been nervous and anxious to help the police to discover the truth. It was probable that he knew and was not afraid of any further attempt on his life. But why he should be so sure that he was not in danger was a mystery.

Perhaps the person most noticeably affected by all this was Mrs. Sconer. It was now, she informed her husband. Touch and Go.

"All I have done here," she said forcibly, forgetting Mr. Sconer's minor part in the effort, "is in danger. If this Gets Out it will cause a scandal which may close the school. You know what parents are."

Mr. Sconer had good reason to know what parents were but did not choose to argue.

"Do you realize, Cosmo, that there is a murderer at work? Don't you see that he may strike again, and this time successfully? You should have got rid of Sime as I told you long ago. And please don't tell me he's a good teacher. I warned you and you ignored my warning."

"We don't know he was pushed," said Mr. Sconer. "He may have made that up."

"To injure the school? Far more reason to wish him clear of the place! Such disloyalty. I should like to know *what* you intend to do before it's too late."

Mr. Sconer sounded sulky and cross.

"I have not the slightest idea."

"What about that man who solves mysteries?" asked Mrs. Sconer suddenly.

"Which man?"

"Don't be obtuse, Cosmo. You know the man. Your friend Gorringer was telling you about him."

"Gorringer? Oh, ah, yes." said Mr. Sconer dubiously. He had been at the university with Hugh Gorringer, now the headmaster of a small public school, the Queen's School, Newminster. Gorringer had told him about one of his assistants, Carolus Deene, whose hobby was the investigation of crime at which he had been preternaturally successful.

"Why not ring him up immediately?" suggested Mrs. Sconer. "Tell him we must have his man here at once. A case of life and death."

"I very much doubt if Gorringer would be interested. You may remember that during his last visit when he suggested we might send him some of our boys, you told him we only prepared boys for the more important public schools and had never gone lower than Hurstpierpoint. He was deeply offended."

"Nonsense. He must be made to see that the case is too urgent for him to quibble about the status of his school."

"Gorringer has big ideas of his own and his school's importance. Besides, how do we know that even if he would consider his Senior History Master coming here in the middle of term, this man Deene would not just add to the confusion and upset the Men?"

"Upset the Men! We need desperate remedies, Cosmo. Please telephone Mr. Gorringer immediately."

"My dear. I hardly think. . ."

" I *know*," said Mrs. Sconer, leaving her husband no alternative.

Thus it was that Carolus Deene, in another and very different school more than a hundred miles away, was called out of class on the Wednesday after the attack on Sime. He went casually to answer a summons from his headmaster. The two confronted one another across the vast desk behind which Mr. Gorringer liked to sit as one enthroned. Mr. Gorringer was a large and somewhat pompous man with a fine stock of old-fashioned clichés and a pair of large hairy ears. Carolus, in his forties, was slim and rather adolescent in appearance, an ex-officer of the

Commandos, a widower and the owner of a large private income, who taught because he could not live idly.

"Ah, Deene," said Mr. Gorringer, using one of his more genial forms of greeting. "I wanted a word with you. I have received by telephone a most pressing appeal from an old friend of mine of university days."

He did not specify the university. Carolus nodded.

"He is the proprietor of a preparatory school in the Cotswolds and is in great trouble."

"Financial?"

"No. No. At least I have no reason to think that. He seems to have no difficulty in collecting the most exorbitant fees from the parents of his pupils. No. The trouble is more, I gather, in what I think I may call your line. There has been an attempted murder on his staff."

"I often wonder that school murders are not more frequent," put in Carolus.

"This is not a matter for levity," Mr. Gorringer said sternly. "One of his assistants was impelled by an unknown assailant down the staircase of a church tower and survived by a miracle."

"The boys, you think?"

"No, Deene, I must ask you to be serious. There have been other manifestations of a disturbing nature." Mr. Gorringer gave some details which he had received from Mr. Sconer. "I am really sorry for my friend," ended Mr. Gorringer. "His life-work is threatened."

"You think it worth saving? I don't care much for preparatory schools."

"He has come to me with the most extraordinary proposal. It is nothing less than that you should spend a short period, ostensibly as one of his assistants, on the staff of his school and attempt to elucidate the matter before scandal and ruin overwhelm him."

27

"In the middle of term?" asked Carolus incredulously.

"It is, I know, a most unconventional suggestion. A more hidebound headmaster than I would have dismissed it out-of-hand. But the friendships of our young manhood, Deene, create a strong bond and I felt it my duty at least to put the matter to you."

"What about my Upper Fifth? I've just got some inklings of history into their thick pates."

Mr. Gorringer raised his hand.

"Take no thought of that," he said. "I myself will fill your place for a week or two if you should decide to go to my friend's rescue."

Carolus, for once in his life, was astounded.

"I don't know what to say," he admitted.

"I must warn you of one thing," said Mr. Gorringer. "While Sconer is the best of fellows, he has a wife who . . . In a word, he is not his own master. Mrs. Sconer is what in the crude but expressive parlance of today is known as a battle-axe. During my only visit to St. Asprey's School she found occasion to insult me."

Carolus smiled.

"I think I'll take this on," he said.

"With a full sense of responsibility I say I am glad, Deene. Glad. You will realize, of course, that what we hope, what we expect of you is a solution of the mystery before anything worse may befall. I say that because all too often when you investigate a case—though in the end your sagacity triumphs—there seem to come more disasters. We want no murders here, Deene."

"Or anywhere else, headmaster."

"No. Exactly. Of course. But I am asking you to save the reputation of my friend's school, not to divert yourself with elaborate investigations while greater disasters come to it. I am sure you will. And so God Speed. Deene. I shall welcome you back in triumph within ten days. Yes, I think we must make that the limit."

"I'll see what I can do, headmaster," said Carolus and after obtaining details of the geographical situation of St. Asprey's he went home to prepare his departure.

Chapter Three

On the next day, which was a Thursday, Carolus Deene drove his Bentley Continental to the pretentious pseudo-Elizabethan entrance of St. Asprey's and rang the bell. The air of grandeur of it all was somewhat dispelled when the door was opened by an untidy woman in a plastic apron who was smoking a cigarette and looked at him suspiciously.

"You the new Man?" she asked. "They're expecting you. I say! Is that your car? Well! You better come through to his study."

"Thank you." said Carolus.

"We're all upside down," confided the little woman. "Don't hardly know where we are, with all that's been going on. There's one of the Men laid up with broken legs he got from falling down the church tower—or being pushed, as he says. All I can say is, you be careful of that Matron."

"Really?"

"I should say so. There's nothing she misses and it all goes back to Mrs. Sconer. So if you want to stay you better keep on the right side of her. I wouldn't trust any of them, myself. All at one another's throats. It quite gives you the creeps, the things that are happening."

"So I understand. May I ask your name?"

"I'm Mrs. Skippett. I come to work here daily, though its more for something to do, because there's not much going on in the village. Don't take any notice of Her, by the way. She's All Talk."

"Who?"

"Mrs. Sconer, I mean. She's very high and mighty but not when it Comes To It. I always say her bark's worse than her bite, though she's got Him under her thumb all right. Still, you don't want to hear that. You'll know all about it in time when you've been here a few days. Only you mind your p's and q's with that Matron. She's the one."

"I'll remember that."

"Something happened last night," went on Mrs. Skippett. "I haven't got to hearing what it was yet, but you can tell by their faces this morning. It won't be long before I find out, either. I shouldn't be surprised if it was something to do with Sime. He's got a trick of looking at you—well! I always say he's Not Right. It's no wonder, with the way the boys carry on sometimes—they're enough to turn you dizzy. But you'll know all about it in time."

Carolus was looking out of the window and saw across the lawn a row of large round objects on stands.

"What are they?" he asked Mrs. Skippett.

"Them? Oh, it's this archery that's all the craze with them this term. Talk about the boys having crazes, the Men are worse. if you ask me. Shooting arrows like so many wild Indians. I don't see the sense of it myself. There they are every afternoon at target practice, as they call it. Robin

Hood and his merry men, my husband calls them but that's something he has seen on the telly."

"I wonder who started this craze," said Carolus.

"It was Mr. Kneller done that."

"One of the Men?"

"No. To tell you the truth he's come here to do the cooking. You wouldn't think that because he's more of a gentleman than any of them if the truth were told. Only his wife was brought up in one of the school cottages before this *was* a school, and she lost her sight in America where they were together and *would* have it that the only place she could feel her way about was this cottage she'd known as a girl, if you see what I mean. So her husband came to see Mr. Sconer and asked him about it and Mr. Sconer told him he had to keep that cottage for when one of the Men was married. It seems that Mr. Kneller had made a hobby of cooking and that, and Mrs. Sconer was only too glad to get rid of the party she had then because Matron said she Drank and was very extravagant with things, though I didn't see it. So it was all arranged and Mr. Kneller came here last term to do the cooking and seems to like it. He's a real gentleman and keeps himself to himself except when he brought out all these bows and arrows he had from America and started them all on it. Next term it will be something else, I daresay. Well, this won't do. I've got my stairs to finish. You'll be all right if you keep out of the way of Matron and don't have too much to do with any of them. But what you *will* find is that they're all half scared of something. It gives me the shudders when I think of it. No one seems to know what'll happen next, what with one thing and another. You heard about that dog having its throat cut? Well, there you are."

Carolus was to find that this was no exaggeration. Fear had entered that community and could not be concealed. As he came to know the Men he found that in each of them this fear took a different form, except in the bedridden Sime who did not seem afraid of anything. Mrs. Sconer, he discovered, feared chiefly for her school and did not feel threatened personally, but Duckmore, a small nervous man with a high forehead and popping eyes, seemed to fear for his life.

Sconer himself, as Carolus found during his interview with him on that first afternoon was in a state of considerable tension. Carolus expected to receive his confidence, but he gained the impression that his visit was not altogether welcome.

"It was Mrs. Sconer who suggested that you might be able to help us," he said. "I think it will be best if I leave you to gather the nature of our troubles for yourself. Anything I might say might give you preconceived ideas."

"That's all right." said Carolus.

"None of the other Men know you are here for anything but to take Sime's classes while he's laid up. But I'm afraid your very noticeable motorcar may make them think otherwise. We must hope for the best about that. Here is a copy of our timetable. . ."

"How long have you employed Sime?"' asked Carolus curtly.

"Three years now. He's a very clever teacher."

"Did you know he was in the habit of going up to the top of the church tower with field glasses?"

"I *had* heard some rumour of it." Sconer fidgetted with the edge of his handkerchief. "It is not my policy to interfere with the Men more than I can help."

"Even if you suspect them of spying on one another?"

"I had no reason to think anything of the sort. Sime is a most reliable man. I have every confidence in him."

"But not in all your staff?"

"Oh yes. I think so. Parker has been here since the early days of the school. I have always regarded him as my right-hand man and his loyalty to me and the school has never been questioned. Stanley seems very sound—my wife has great confidence in him. Duckmore has an honours degree. He is a trifle highly strung, perhaps, but an excellent teacher. Young Mayring is a splendid coach. We have one lady teacher, Mollie Westerly—most patient and painstaking with the smaller boys."

"You also have a gentleman cook, I understand."

Sconer looked startled.

"I don't remember telling Gorringer anything about that."

"No? Does it work out well?"

"Oh, very. Very. Very good chap. First-rate cook. Mrs. Sconer is delighted with him."

"Keen on archery, isn't he?"

"Archery, yes. Quite a mania with the staff this term. A most healthy sport."

"You don't go in for it yourself?"

"No. No. I haven't the time, unfortunately. Large correspondence, you know. Many responsibilities. But I approve."

Carolus was about to ask more when Sconer jumped up.

"Anything else I think you had better ask the other Men. I don't want to give you predispositions. But first I must introduce you to Mrs. Sconer. We shall find her in the drawing-room, I think. Come along."

Mr. Sconer seemed in a hurry to escape. His wife was in the drawing-room and came forward with a queenly smile to greet Carolus. When the introductions had been made Sconer hurried out.

"Mr. Deene, I am delighted that you have come. I feel you are going to save us."

"It's not as bad as that, surely?"

34

"It could scarcely be worse. We are very near to despair —and next week the school sports will bring all the parents down. My husband does not seem to realize the seriousness of the situation."

"I think he does, Mrs. Sconer. I couldn't help feeling that he is suffering from strain."

"I can't get him to act for our protection. Sime should have been dismissed long ago."

"But he's very efficient, I understand."

"He has a most pernicious influence. My husband seems entirely under his spell. The boys run after him in a most ridiculous way. Matron tells me that when he takes a walk on Sunday the boys compete to walk with him."

"His 'sides are bagged'," said Carolus smiling as he remembered his preparatory school.

"Then our silly young lady teacher seems hypnotized by him. Although Jim Stanley, the best Man we've got is quite mad about her."

"These things are unaccountable, surely?"

"It was just the same with our previous mistress, a woman called O'Maverick. Sime never left her in peace. I insisted on her being dismissed."

"How long ago was that?"

"Mollie Westerly came here this term."

"And what happend to Miss O'Maverick?"

Mrs. Sconer stiffened somewhat.

"I haven't the remotest idea." she said emphatically.

Carolus looked at her, noting this sudden chill, then asked disconcertingly—"Does your Matron know why I am here?"

"I certainly haven't told her," said Mrs. Sconer. "But I should not be surprised if she knew. There is very little she misses. A most competent woman. You heard about the disgusting trick that was played on her? Someone must

35

have a diseased mind to do such a thing. The poor woman was terribly upset. We are looking to you to discover who can have been guilty."

"I should like to have a talk with your Matron."

"I will take you up to her room after lunch," promised Mrs. Sconer. "You will find her a remarkable person."

"Thank you. You have one very young master, I believe?"

"Mayring, yes. Quite a youth, really. He only left Cranleigh last term. Or was it Blundell's? He caused a lot of trouble by bringing his dog here. My husband should never have allowed it. Just as I've repeatedly asked my husband to stop all this archery that is going on."

"A very harmless sport, I should have thought."

"When the school is in its present state of unrest I do *not* think it wise that the Men should be playing with lethal weapons. I understand that an arrow can penetrate at sixty yards. There might be an accident."

"What you mean, surely, is that something might happen which was *not* an accident."

Mrs. Sconer blinked at Carolus.

"You don't think. . ."

"Not necessarily. But that is what *you* think might happen, isn't it Mrs. Sconer?"

"Anything may happen, unless you can get at the truth quickly."

"The truth is not always very welcome, I fear."

Mrs. Sconer thoughtfully left this point and took Carolus to his quarters. the spare room from which Matron had been winkled with some difficulty after her resort to it on the night of the dead rat. It was then time for lunch.

"I have put you at the senior boys' table," Mrs. Sconer said. "I thought it would be less tiresome for you though I'm afraid they all ask questions."

36

"I do myself," admitted Carolus.

At lunch he sat at the head of a table of nine boys of twelve and thirteen who at first watched him covertly while they gobbled their roast mutton then, through the oldest of them whose name he found was Chavanne, began a thorough cross-examination.

"Please sir, is that your car in the drive?"

"It is."

"Is it a Bentley Continental 1966 model?"

"Yes."

There was a moment's respite while Chavanne turned to his neighbour to say—"Told you so. Sucks to you."

Then—"Do you play cricket, sir?"

Carolus forgot himself.

"No. Detest the game."

This was a set-back to them all since they were seeking, as small boys will, suitable grounds for hero-worship.

"Were you at Oxford or Cambridge, sir?"

"Oxford."

"Did you get your blue?"

This was almost too much to hope for. Even Mr. Sime, the most popular master, had only been to Manchester University and had no athletic distinctions.

"Half blue," admitted Carolus.

"Good Lord, sir, did you really? What was it for, sir?"

"Boxing," said Carolus.

Another boy joined in. It seemed almost too much for Chavanne alone.

"Were you in the war, sir?"

"Yes. For a time."

"Army or Air Force, sir? Or was it"—hope seemed to rise—"the Navy?"

"Army," said Carolus flatly. "Now for goodness' sake eat your pudding."

But the two asked at once—"What regiment, sir?" And when Carolus said the Commandos there was a long thoughtful silence. He took advantage of this to say he would answer no more questions, but he had said enough. His interrogaters were impatient to spread their news broadcast. Sime's status was already in jeopardy.

After lunch he was taken by Mrs. Sconer to Matron's Room, half sitting-room, half surgery, which was impregnated with the smell of medicines. Matron herself, looking spare and toothy, unwillingly turned for a moment from the window at which she had been standing and asked Carolus if he would like a cup of tea, explaining that it was a little treat Mrs. Sconer allowed her after lunch. Carolus declined and watched while Matron poured out, her attention continually returning to the window.

Carolus asked a few enticing questions but for a long time seemed unable to release the flood of information that he believed was here. But when he mentioned the dead rat Matron's hollow cheeks flushed.

"If it had not been for the sake of the school I should have gone to the police." she said.

"You have no idea who it might be?"

Matron had many ideas.

"It was one of the Men," she said. "No boy would have had such a nasty mind. I wouldn't put it past any of those we've got now, except Mr. Stanley. He would never have done a thing like that. I shouldn't be surprised if it was that young Mayring. He's been impertinent to me once this term already. I had to complain to Mrs. Sconer about it. I've just seen him go across to the pavilion."

"What does that suggest?" asked Carolus innocently.

"Nothing, only you have to notice things. He might have done it. Or Duckmore. I've had a lot of trouble with Duckmore. I was telling Mrs. Sconer, we ought never to have had him here. Too excitable altogether. I can quite believe it of him. And he has behaved very strangely with me since Mrs. Sconer found out about his bill at the village stores. Well, I felt she ought to know. Or Sime, of course. Sime's just the sort of man to do a thing like that. There's Mayring now, coming back from the pavilion." Her eyes had been turning aside at intervals not to lose touch with events outside the window. "I wonder what he's been over there for. Yes, Sime could have done it. We know all about *him*. Mrs. Sconer would have got rid of him years ago if Mr. Sconer did not have such faith in him as a master."

"What other suspects have you?" asked Carolus.

"There's Mr. Kneller who does the cooking," said Matron. Carolus noticed that while 'the Men' got their unadorned surnames, this anomalous member of the staff was Mister. "Ever since I felt it my duty to tell Mrs. Sconer about the eggs, he has tried to be unpleasant with me. Then there's Parker."

"Yes?"

"He's been here a long time and all that, but I felt Mrs. Cconer should know he was spending his time down at the Windmill Inn and coming back fuddled at night. You'd think he was too old for that sort of behaviour but with the Men we've got now you never know. Then I suppose it could have been someone from outside, and Horlick the gardener had brought flowers into the house that day."

"You're sure it was a man?" asked Carolus.

"No, I'm not," Matron said sharply. "I see Chavanne's just gone up to Sime's window. The boys seem quite silly about that man. I must tell Mrs. Sconer this—Chavanne stands gossiping with Sime for hours on end. No, I'm *not* sure it was a man, though how any woman, even Mollie Westerly, could bring herself to touch the thing I can't

39

imagine. Then we've one or two women who come in for cleaning, Mrs. Horlick the gardener's wife is one."

"What about my friend Mrs. Skippett?"

Matron stared.

"Have you spoken to her?" she asked. "I don't know when you had the chance. I saw her go off on her bicycle before lunch. She talks a lot, of course, and ever since that came out about her husband she's blamed me for Mrs. Sconer knowing, so I suppose she might have done it for vengeance. She's here, there and everywhere about the house and I can't always keep track of what she's doing. I can't say I like the woman but I don't somehow think it was her. For all the chattering she does I don't think she's malicious. Mrs. Horlick, who always claims to be an angel, is far more likely to have done something really spiteful, like that. But you never know. That's Mollie Westerly now, going off with Stanley again. I told Mrs. Sconer that ought to be stopped. Only we think quite a lot of Stanley—he's a nice quiet fellow. I suppose Sime can see them going from his room."

"You haven't mentioned Mr. Sconer himself," said Carolus. "As a suspect, I mean."

Was it a smile which stretched Matron's thin lips over her dentures?

"He'd never *dare*," she said finally, and left it at that.

Chapter Four

Carolus wandered out on to the lawn on which the St. Asprey's Archery Club, as the Men had begun to call themselves, practised their sport. A little thatched summerhouse stood in a corner of the lawn near what he took to be the shooting base and in his restless inquisitive way Carolus peered into it. He was surprised to find a tall man examining an arrow.

Denis Kneller looked like an old-fashioned colonial, his tanned face, bright blue eyes and large pipe suggesting camp-fires and trapping, or diamond mines, or tea-planting in faraway places. He spoke slowly, too, and moved deliberately as though profoundly concerned with what he was doing.

He looked up at Carolus without hostility.

"You're the new Man, I take it." he said, thrusting forward a brown hand. "I'm the cook."

There was a hint of defiance in this self-introduction.

"I hear you're very keen on all this," said Carolus nodding towards the arrows.

"So, so," said Denis Kneller with marked casualness. But Carolus saw the eyes blaze with the unmistakable light of fanaticism and knew that he had touched on an obsession. He was willing to learn for there seemed to him something occult, almost mythical about the whole business of archery, but he would like to have obtained information by his own questions instead of hearing a slow, not over-articulate discourse delivered between puffs from Kneller's pipe. When Kneller began to talk in a way that pre-supposed understanding from Carolus of 'the Royal Tox', Carolus stopped him.

"What's that?" he asked.

The Royal Toxophilite Society, it appeared and Carolus learned that the Prince Regent had been its patron, and was still remembered in 'the Prince's lengths' (100 yards, 80 yards and 60 yards. still used in the championships) and the 'Prince's reckoning' for the values of the rings of the target, from the gold centre which scored nine, red seven, blue five, black three and the white outer ring one. Kneller further explained that an 'end' consisted of six arrows shot in two groups, and what was a 'York round' and an 'American round'. It was all very esoteric.

Carolus asked what was the distance of the target here and Kneller explained that as Mollie Westerly was a keen archer they did not use the greater ranges which in men's championships were as long as a hundred yards. "But", he said, "the thing is to be able to shoot at different ranges from thirty to eighty yards, say. We can't manage more than sixty here. The targets are standing at forty now."

"It looks enormous to me," admitted Carolus.

"Not really," Kneller told him seriously. "They've become very keen, you know, and some of them are quite good. There's a couple who live in the neighbourhood, Bill Ferris and his wife, parents of one of the boys, who come over most afternoons and are really up to championship standard. Ferris learned to shoot in Belgium which gives him a different kind of accuracy."

"Why?"

"*Tir à la perche*," explained Kneller. "They shoot there at dummy wooden birds with plumes on them perched on the crossarms of a thirty-five metre mast. On its top is the king bird the, *coq*, and there are big and small birds at different heights. The archers shoot straight upwards with very heavy arrows called *maquets* and have to dislodge the birds. This gives them altogether a greater facility. Shooting at a target on the ground is apt to make you proficient only at certain lengths and marks. Those who practice *tir à perche* are more versatile."

"Yes, I can imagine that. From what wood are bows made nowadays?"

"Yew," said Kneller emphatically. "By tradition and in fact. It is as it always has been the best wood for the bow."

"What about field archery? Does anyone in civilized countries try to kill wild animals with a bow and arrow?"

"I should think they do!" said Kneller enthusiastically. "A man named Saxton Pope in America made friends with Ishi, the last of the Yana Indians who taught him all he knew. Pope and another professor, Arthur Young, proved that most game animals could be killed by bow and arrow. They killed grizzly bear and moose, and Young achieved the believed impossible by killing the great Kodiak bear with a single shot. Then they went to Africa and shot lions. Extraordinary, really."

"Quite," said Carolus. "Surely it couldn't be done with arrows like these?"

"You use a hunting arrow or broadhead," said Kneller, unscrewing the head from the arrow he held. "Wait, I've got some here and will show you. I was a member of the N.F.A.A. in America and have always been more interested in hunting than in target shooting. Look at this—heavier, more fletching and with a steel tip of razor sharpness."

"Dangerous looking thing, that."

"A man would have to be a good shot to put it to any effective use," said Kneller. "But we've worked out a field round with targets of various sizes and go round it like a golf course on Sundays."

"Who are your best shots?"

"Young Mayring's getting pretty good, and Bill Ferris's wife Stella. Mollie Westerly's very accurate on the target at one range, forty yards, but gets lost at other lengths. Jim Stanley—very nice chap on the staff who suffers from being popular with Mrs. Sconer—has come on wonderfully. I've interested him in field archery now and he 'killed' a wooden hare at twenty yards last Sunday. Dear old Jumbo Parker's not much good but he likes to come out with us. But Duckmore is a mystery. He doesn't seem to be able to hit the target yet he has got the manner of a skilled professional and has the whole vocabulary of archery at his fingertips. He seems to be suffering from a strain of some sort; I think he may have been good once, but you need calm and peace of mind to be good at this."

"That completes your membership?"

"Yes. Horlick, the gardener, who's a bit of a character likes to try his luck sometimes when he's not being watched from Matron's window. But that's not often. That window overlooks the range and if you've met Matron you'll know that she doesn't miss much."

"Nothing, I should imagine. Does she approve of archery?"

"Matron approves of nothing," said Kneller. "But that is not of prime importance. She is merely an observation post. And now with Sime laid up we are watched from two quarters. His bed commands an excellent view of us."

The two had come out of the summer-house now and Carolus looked at the school buildings.

"Which is Sime's room?" he asked.

"That," said Kneller, indicating a white bungalow, "is the staff quarters. There are four bedrooms there and the common-room. As you see it's joined by a passage with the main house. Sime, Stanley, Duckmore and Mayring sleep in the staff bungalow and we send along coffee at eleven and tea at four o'clock to the common-room. Mollie Westerly and Matron have rooms in the private part of the house, so has Jumbo Parker who was here before the bungalow was built. That's Sime's window with a crowd of small boys round it." He indicated a window some yards from where they stood. "I suppose they've put you in the spare room next to Matron's?"

"Yes."

A smartly dressed man and woman appeared by a garden path. The man was burly and tweed-clad, a prosperous-looking fellow in his early fifties, the woman, also in tweeds had a good complexion and an attractive smile. At a distance she looked very young but when they approached Carolus saw that she might not be much younger than her husband though fresh-looking and attractive. Kneller introduced him to Mr. and Mrs. Ferris.

"You're standing in for Sime, I take it?" said Bill Ferris with a friendly smile.

"Yes, for a week or two."

"Bad luck his being laid up."

"I rather gathered it was good luck that he wasn't killed," said Carolus.

"Yes. See what you mean. D'you go in for this archery stuff of ours?"

45

"I never have. It looks as though I must make a start. You're all pretty keen, I hear."

"Gets the old tum down." said Bill Ferris. "Or so Stella tells me."

"It doesn't seem to have done much for you," said Stella smiling.

Pleasant, cultured, upper middle class, wealthy, country-dwelling English people, Carolus thought; well mannered, probably hospitable and, one would suppose, the soul of honour. What was it he did not like about them? Bill's rich resounding voice? Stella's pearls? Or something watchful and tense in both of them?

"How's Sime?" Bill asked Kneller.

"I haven't seen him. He's *eating* all right," said Kneller sharply.

Bill looked across at Sime's window.

"I see my youngster's among the worshippers at the shrine," he said peevishly.

"Oh darling, what's it matter?" asked Stella. "There's always a popular master at every school."

"Yes. but why *Sime?*" He turned to Kneller. "Anything else happened?"

"There was a row in Sime's room last night. It started as an argument about the Second Eleven, I believe and grew into an almighty shindy between Sime, Stanley and Mayring. But that's nothing unusual."

Mollie Westerly appeared, looking, Carolus thought, very unlike any schoolmistress he had seen. She was in her middle twenties, cool, rather lovely in a Mediterranean way and her clothes had that simple-appropriate look of quality which can only be achieved at great expense. She gave Carolus a polite smile but said almost at once—"Why haven't we started? It's half past two."

The crowd of boys round Sime's window had been

drawn away by the main body on its way to the cricket field.

Mollie's brisk decisiveness semed to animate Kneller and Bill and Stella Ferris for bows were produced and practice began. This was not a casual affair—each took six arrows and shot them all at his own target—then all four walked down to retrieve their arrows chattering about the sport as all practicants of all sports do. There did not seem much difference between their respective skills. Stella Ferris was the only one who missed the target altogether with one arrow. Kneller had the highest score.

Carolus watched while the process was repeated and noted how orderly it all was. They might have been governed by the strong rules which are obeyed at rifle butts, and for the same reason—to avoid any possibility of accident. The bow and arrow were still, after all, as lethal as at Crecy.

"Like to try?" Kneller asked him.

"I would, but not today." Carolus said.

Kneller sat with him on a bench while the other three continued their practice.

"You find it interesting?"

"Of course. I've never considered it except historically, you know. I suppose the invention of the bow ranks almost with making fire and using speech as a step forward in human progress. It really put mankind on top of the animal world, didn't it?"

"I've never thought of that. It was certainly the most accurate way of projecting a missile till firearms came."

"But not the only way."

"No. The sling, the boomerang, the blow-pipe, the dart. . ."

"*And*, of course, other forms of catapult projection. It must have suggested those."

47

Kneller did not seem much interested, but Carolus, watching him, went on.

"The crossbow was a kind of catapult, wasn't it? But the Greeks used an enormous engine called a ballista, I seem to remember, which could hurl great rocks and beams with remarkable accuracy. I am sorry that this kind of thing has sunk to the mere schoolboy's catapult. I should like ballista-firing to be revived."

"It couldn't have the appeal of archery," said Kneller briefly.

"I don't know. It wouldn't be difficult to construct a rough implement, powerful enough to hurl a rock some yards at a given object. It could be pretty accurate, too. If it did not kill, it could impel. . ."

"I suppose you're pulling my leg," said Kneller slowly. "It would have nothing to do with archery."

"No," agreed Carolus, "except that one was a later development of the other and suggested by it. Look, I think I should go over and make the acquaintance of the man I am replacing. How do I find his room?"

Kneller told him the way.

"Go into the staff bungalow there by that green door. Sime's room is on your left, number 3."

Carolus found Sime propped up in a bed facing the window. His appearance was not prepossessing. He had a rather brutal and beefy face with small cunning pig's eyes and a thick neck. It was the face of a big man but Carolus would have been surprised to know that Sime was six foot two in height as in fact he was. He looked up surprised when Carolus, after a tap entered, but seemed to guess Carolus's identity and gave him a grudging smile as he put down the Dennis Wheatley novel he was reading.

"You've come to take over my job, I gather," he said. "I

wish you luck with the little fiends. But I don't think it will be long before I'm on my feet."

"I hope not," said Carolus politely. "What a piece of bad luck for you. You must hate being laid up in this lovely weather."

"It wasn't a matter of luck. Some bastard pushed me down that staircase."

Carolus showed no particular curiosity, only a polite concern.

"It was at the church, wasn't it? Some of these old tower staircases are dangerous."

Sime seemed exasperated.

"Nothing to do with the staircase. It was the push I'd got. I'd just driven up on my way to Cheltenham, and thought I'd take a look at the view from the tower. Then *this* had to happen."

"You weren't able to drive home afterwards of course."

"No. They had to bring my car. I'd left it at the gate. I wonder they didn't find a charge to make about that. It was out there all night. It's that *push* I can't get over, though."

"Really? Did you actually feel that?"

"Of course I did. The hell of a great thump in the small of the back. However, you want to know about these classes of mine."

For twenty minutes Sime gave a resumé of his programme and Carolus wondered how he had gained the reputation of a brilliant teacher for he seemed to be behind all his schedules and had very little understanding of his pupils' young individualities. He seemed to take it for granted that Carolus would be as little interested as he was in them. When he finished Carolus tried a more general approach.

"School seems in a bit of a mess," he said.

Sime looked up quickly.

"In what way?"

"Atmosphere," said Carolus vaguely. "Everyone seems half scared."

"All a lot of nonsense. Some half-wit playing practical jokes. *I'm* the only one who has a right to be scared and I'm not at all."

Suddenly Carolus dived forward from where he sat and pulled from under Sime's pillow a ·22 revolver, the butt of which he had just seen protruding.

"Then why have you got this?"

He watched Sime's face. He saw an angry contortion of the features change almost instantly to a grin.

"It's no business of yours," said Sime equably. "But I don't mind satisfying your curiosity. (Rather cheek, you know, pulling that out.) I like firearms. Got quite a collection at home. Bought that in a pub in London last holidays. I shouldn't be surprised if it had been used in hold-ups. But I did not want anyone to find it while I was laid up. That's all."

Carolus thought it wise to appear to accept this. He wanted Sime's confidence and thought now that his own move had been ill-advised. So he did not mention what he had seen—that it was loaded. He handed it back.

"Sorry," he said. "It *was* a bit cheeky, as you say. I like firearms myself."

They talked amicably for a few minutes more, then Carolus asked if Sime was comfortable, right in front of a window.

"I don't mind, really. It was that bitch Matron who had my bed moved here. Said it was easier for the doctor. I suppose she thinks everyone is as inquisitive as she is. All I can see from here is that ridiculous archery. "

"You don't go in for it?"

50

"Kids sport. I'm not a blasted Red Indian. The rest of the staff has gone mad on it."

"So it seems."

"I hadn't time, anyway. I wanted to get a decent cricket eleven together. Young Mayring's quite good but I'm responsible for the cricket here. It takes time, coaching the little beggars."

Carolus stood up to go.

"I say, would you do me a favour?" Sime asked. "I want a letter posted and can't rely on any of the lot here."

"I'll certainly post it."

Sime handed him a stamped and adressed envelope.

"Stick it in your pocket," he said. "This inquisitive crowd we've got would want to know all about it."

Carolus did so.

"You going in to staff tea? The common room's next door. You'll find them all there presently."

When he was out of Sime's room Carolus looked at the letter. If this had been a murder case he would not have scrupled to read the contents but in the circumstances he did not feel justified in doing so. But he noted the name and address on it—Mrs. Ricks, 22 Sapperton Road, Cheltenham.

Chapter Five

It was still to early for staff tea and wandering outside again Carolus met a genial-looking elderly man who was coming from the direction of the archery lawn. He guessed it was Jumbo Parker.

The Oldest Member of the staff greeted him in a friendly way, complained of the rheumatism which was causing him to walk in a stiff-legged way, and suggested that they should go in together and wait in the master's common-room for tea.

"It will be along in a minute," he said. "I must say Mrs. Skippett's never late. You go in and I'll join you."

The common-room had a well-worn look, curtains, chair-covers and some shreds of Axminster carpet were all near their end. There were armchairs but one was of creaking wickerwork and the springs in another had ceased to co-operate. The smell of pipe smoke, some piles of exercise books, a bottle of red ink on a stained table-cloth through which the deal of the table was visible—it was all in the narrowest convention of preparatory school common-rooms.

Carolus had to wait some minutes for Jumbo Parker but as he had predicted the tea soon came and Parker poured his own tea into a breakfast cup. The other cups were generous, but this was a giant mug and in a moment Carolus guessed that it was one of those privileges achieved by Jumbo Parker for his two decades at the school. Parker handed him one of the other cups then helped himself liberally to bread and jam.

"I guessed you were the new Man," he said chuckling as though it were a joke. "In spite of your dashing motorcar. Then I saw you at lunch. I noticed that oaf Chavanne was pestering you with questions. You shouldn't allow it."

"No?"

"You'll soon realize that," said the jovial old boy with a touch of patronage. "If you give the little fiends an inch they take an ell. Especially this Satan's brood we've got here."

"Worse than others?"

"Not really," admitted Parker. "Only in the middle of term one is apt to think so. Do help yourself to more tea. The other Men will be here in a minute. I expect they're just shooting an end each before coming in."

"An end?"

"I understand that's the correct term in archery."

Young Mayring, in immaculate flannels, appeared and was introduced to Carolus. He would have been a good-looking young man if his eyes had not been set too close together.

"Finished with your delinquents?" asked Parker, smiling again.

"Yes. The hell-hounds were infuriating this afternoon. That moron Crestley. . ."

"Oh yes. Crestley. I have the cretin for French. Certifiable, isn't he?"

"He was trying to tell that imbecile Metcalf how to play an off-break. . ."

"You going to take Sime in his tea?" asked Parker suddenly and more seriously.

"I will, yes," replied Mayring as though he were undertaking a sacred duty.

He got together bread and butter and some jam on a plate and took them, with a cup of tea from the room.

"Have you met Sime?" asked Parker.

"Yes. I've been chatting with him."

Carolus saw that Parker was watching him, as if to gather something from his manner, but Carolus added no comment. Parker turned his attention to Mayring when he returned. He was evidently expecting a bulletin.

"Still raving about Stanley," Mayring said. "It seems some of the little reptiles who came to his window today told him what Stanley is supposed to have said to that half-wit Thompson. Some other lunatic heard Matron telling Mrs. Sconer what Sime said when Stanley repeated Sconer's remark about Duckmore."

Jumbo Parker semed able to follow this, even to enjoy it.

"It's a good thing Matron doesn't know what the little stinkers in the Lower Fifth told me when they heard what Mollie Westerly thought about it."

Mayring made a sound indicating scorn and incredulity.

" 'Matron doesn't know'!" he said. "Famous last words."

Duckmore came in. Prematurely bald and grey, with prominent eyes and a neurotic twitch, he seemed amiable but preoccupied.

"Where have you been, Ducks?" asked Parker. "Oh, you had the junior game this afternoon. How did the scum behave?"

"I had to send that clot Farraway off the field," said Duckmore unhappily.

"Why? What did the monster do?" asked Mayring.

"Showing off again."

"He's a mongol really, you know. The other animals in that crowd are bad enough but Farraway is beyond hope."

Someone was at the door and the heads of all the Men immediately turned towards it. Carolus noticed this, then and thereafter. Everybody at St. Asprey's seemed to be waiting for something. Every movement, every approach caused curiosity, expectancy, even alarm. But it was only Jim Stanley, a nondescript man with prominent ears, but some pretension to good looks.

"I've just scored 35," he said, before he noticed Carolus. "My very first arrow . . . oh, how d'you do? You're taking Sime's place?"

"Temporarily," said Carolus.

"I wish it were for good," Stanley said frankly and raised a little muted laughter.

"I'll see if he wants any more tea," said Mayring and went out.

"What's Mayring being so obliging for?" asked Stanley. "Let him come and get his tea. Or why don't some of the little horrors who hang round his window get it for him? I saw that clod-pate Chavanne there as I came in with some other numskulls. I sent the whole crowd indoors. Who's taking Prep, tonight?"

"It's my turn," said Mayring, who had returned.

"Will you see that blockhead Munson does his Latin prose, then? The little thug hasn't looked at it for three nights."

"I certainly will. I was going to send that idle mooncalf to the study myself today."

They were interrupted by a loud banging. Duckmore sat up straight and said—"What's that?" in a startled voice.

"Sime," said Parker. "He wants something."

"Run along, Mayring," Stanley jibed. "You're his nurse, aren't you?"

Mayring flushed.

"Someone else can go this time," he said.

The banging was renewed. Without a word, Duckmore left them. There was silence in the room as everyone waited. When he came back he was carrying a plate and empty cup.

"He wants to speak to you, Stanley," he said nervously. "He's raging because you sent the boys away from his window."

Stanley rose.

"I'll soon settle that," he said ferociously and went out, leaving the door open.

"Oh God, another row," said Mayring.

He was right, and most of it, the shouted part, was audible from the common-room.

"What do you mean by sending those boys away from my window? Of all the damned impudence!"

Stanley sounded cool.

"They had no business to be there. They were supposed to be getting ready for tea."

"What the hell's it to do with you? You're not on duty today. You think just because you suck up to those bitches you can do what you like in this place."

"You won't last long, Sime. You may not realize it but your days are numbered."

"Oh *are* they? Then let me tell you something which you'd know sooner or later. I'm buying a partnership in this school. So we'll see who will last. If you think that you or any of your crowd will be about here after I get control, you're a bigger fool than I thought you."

It sounded as though the shot had gone home.

"A partnership?" said Stanley.

"You heard. If not the whole shooting-match. Then you'll see if Mrs. Sconer can help you. And in future when I'm talking to any of the boys, you leave them alone."

Stanley looked shaken when he returned to the common-room.

"Did you hear what he said?" he asked.

"I shouldn't take much notice of that," said Parker equably. "I've heard these stories before. He hasn't got the money and if he had the Sconers would never sell."

"He seemed very confident about it. I'm sure he's got some hold here we know nothing about."

"Nonsense. It's the usual bluff. But you'd better not tell Kneller about it. You know what he is—believes every-thing. If he thought he might lose that cottage he'd go rav-ing mad. It's the only place in which his wife can live and Sime can't bear either of them."

Cigarettes were lit now and Jumbo Parker pulled at his pipe. There was a noise like a faulty wireless set at full blast outside which was explained by Parker.

"The zoo's loose," he said. "The little savages were not long at tea today. Who's on duty before prep?"

There was no reply to this and Carolus guessed that it was Sime's turn and therefore, perhaps, his.

"Was it Sime's?" he asked.

"As a matter of fact it was," said Parker. "But you can't go among those dregs yet. You must get to know the horrible little reprobates before chancing your life among them at this time of the day. They're always at their most villainous when they're let out after tea. It's supposed to be their own recreation time."

"I don't mind," said Carolus, rather amused.

The noise increased.

"Someone'll have to control the little devils," said May-ring. "or they'll pull the place to pieces in front of Matron's eyes. Not that much isn't in front of Matron's eyes and if it happened behind her back she'd manage to see it."

"I'll go," said Stanley. "I want to see none of the little sinners get round that window. Partnership! If it *is* true I I shouldn't dream of staying here, and if it isn't true Sime will be out at the end of this term. I can tell you that."

He slammed the door behind him.

"And *he* should know," Mayring said bitterly. "He was in Matron's room again today."

The wild noise outside the window receded and the atmosphere in the common-room grew more confidential, if not more cosy.

"You must think this a strange sort of school," said Jumbo Parker to Carolus. "It used not to be. There was a very pleasant atmosphere until a term or two ago. I'm afraid everyone's rather on edge at present."

"Yes. I heard about some of the dark happenings. Have there been any more since Sime was laid up?"

Carolus saw that his disingenuous question had produced marked effect. The faces of all three Men were turned to him with startled expressions though whether their surprise was assumed or not he could not tell.

"Now you come to mention it, no," said Parker.

"My God! Do you really think. . ." began Mayring.

"It's only five days," Duckmore almost pleaded. "It's too early to say."

"If I thought. . ." Mayring struck the palm of his hand with his fist and turning to Carolus said—"You know my puppy was killed?"

"I heard so, yes."

"I'd murder the swine who did it."

"I shouldn't talk like that, if I were you," Carolus told him.

They were all silenced again by the sound of knocking,

58

gentle this time and on the door of the neighbouring room. They waited without speaking to see if they could gather who it was. This was easy, for Sime had a penetrating voice.

"Hullo, Mollie," they heard him say, but before she had answered the door was closed again.

"Good thing Stanley isn't here," said Mayring. "And by the way, Stella Ferris went across to the window to talk to him this afternoon. Yes, right in front of Bill. You should have seen his face."

Nobody answered but it seemed that both Parker and Duckmore were thinking it over. At last Parker rose slowly from the wicker armchair and Carolus was relieved that the gathering broke up.

He wanted to do what he had done in every case he had investigated—visit the local pub. He had rarely failed to learn something of interest there. Sometimes the publican himself was informative, sometimes he employed a chatty barmaid, sometimes he heard odd facts or opinions from the customers. In any case, short of receiving confidences which he did not yet expect, he had heard all he expected from the Men and wanted a breather. So much intrigue and suspicion was oppressive.

The Windmill Inn was nearly a mile away but as it was the only licensed premises in a radius of more than four miles it was sure to be 'the local' for those members of the staff who like to visit a pub. It was now twenty to six so Carolus decided to walk the distance. This would give him some exercise and bring him to the Windmill promptly at opening time.

He waited till he was some way from the school before learning the way from a postman. This reminded him of Sime's letter and hearing that there was a letter-box in the village he posted it. When he reached the Windmill Inn he found no one on the customer's side of the counter but the landlord stood behind it.

Mr. Pocket was a sprightly little man with an Arnold Bennett quiff of hair and a clipped bristly reddish moustache.

"Hullo! Where have you sprung from?" he asked Carolus.

"I walked across."

"Thought I didn't hear a car pull up." he seemed to realize what Carolus had said and asked—"Across from where?"

"St. Asprey's."

This seemed a big relief to him.

"Oh, you're the New Man come to take Sime's place till he can get about again. Arrive this morning, did you?"

A question-asker, thought Carolus and knew that he was on easy ground. Mr. Pocket might answer questions by asking others but he was bursting with information. Carolus ordered a Scotch and soda.

"How do you like it up there?" asked Mr. Pocket.

"Seems a bit disturbed."

"A *bit*? It must be a shambles after this last go-round. Not that you can be surprised. That Sime's a nasty piece of work. But what are they all scared of? That's what I want to know."

"Are they scared?"

"Scared stiff. When you get grown men come in here trembling like an ash-bin. . ."

Carolus saw the potential start of a new corruption of the language but let it go.

"Really?"

"Face white as chalk and hands jumping like jack-in-the-boxes, then ordering a double brandy, you know something's wrong."

60

"You mean Duckmore?"

"Yes, but the others are not much better. There's old Parker enjoyed his pint here ever since I've been here, hardly ever comes now. Makes you think, doesn't it?"

"Is young Mayring a customer of yours?"

"Oh, yes, he comes over sometimes when he's touched Sconer for a sub. On about his dog being killed most of the time. The one I don't like is Stanley. I can't say why but there it is. You talked to him?"

"A little. He seems all right."

"He may seem all right but from what the rest of them say he's not much. Too thick with the old woman and the matron. And what about Horlick?"

"That's the gardener, isn't it?"

"*He's* a character. You wait till you meet him. *And* his wife."

"I haven't seen either of them yet. Only Mrs. Skippett."

"She's a good sort. Very good to my wife when she was ill. She lives across the way. Yes, you *have* got a bright lot over there. I shouldn't be surprised if something was to happen one of these days."

"Really?"

"Not a little bit, I shouldn't be. What with Sime and that. No one seems to know where they are. I was only saying to the wife. I tell you who does come in, though; that's this fellow they've got as cook. Bit of a mystery, that is. What's *he* doing, cooking? He's not the type, is he? I wouldn't be surprised if there was something behind it. He never says much when he comes in and only drinks mild-and-bitter. I can't make him out. Seems to think the world of his wife, though. I will say that. Terrible misfortune, losing your sight. Have you met her yet?"

"No. I only arrived this morning."

61

"So you said. Well, I wish you luck. I shouldn't like it, with all that Talk."

Carolus invited him to have a drink but he refused.

"I've only just had my tea," he explained. "I wonder some of the boys' parents don't get to hear what's going on. I shouldn't like one of my kids to be mixed up in that. Would you? It can't be healthy, really, when you come to think of it. I thought it was larking at first. There was a lot of that last term when they had a girl there called Sally O'Maverick. She was all for a laugh. They say the old woman got rid of her. She had the looks, you see. Real little beauty, she was. Irish, too. I was sorry to see her go. The men were all mad about her. Even old Parker came out of his shell when she was here. But there you are. The old woman and the matron between them cooked her goose."

"There's a very nice-looking assistant there now."

"Yes, but it's not the same thing. She's got money and thinks a lot of herself. She's never been in here—I've only seen her the once, when I went to church. That Sally was over here two or three times a week and didn't mind joining in a sing-song. Till all of a sudden she stopped coming and at the end of the term I heard she'd gone. There was talk about that, too. Some said she was in the family way. But I wouldn't believe it. She wasn't the sort. Didn't mind a laugh and that but she knew what she was doing."

"No idea where she went?"

"I did hear she was in Cheltenham, only that may be no more than a tale. But this we've had lately's very different to her sort of larking. That rat in Matron's bed I wouldn't have put past Sally, but not the rest of it. Animals being killed and that. You couldn't have wanted a kinder-hearted girl. As for pushing anyone down a flight of stone stairs. . ."

"You think Sime was pushed, then?"

Mr. Pocket stared at Carolus.

"Well, it stands to reason, doesn't it?" he asked.

"I don't see why."

"He *says* he was pushed."

Carolus decided to let the point go. He was surprised to find out how much the publican knew.

"Do you go up to the school?" he asked.

"I can't get out much," said Mr. Pocket. "My wife's away, staying with her sister. But I like to know what's going on."

Like Matron, thought Carolus and had another drink.

Chapter Six

That night Carolus was himself witness to one of those nocturnal incidents which had disturbed the peace of St. Asprey's.

He had learned by now the lay-out of the whole place with its architectural anomalies. The main part of the big house was occupied on its ground floor with class-rooms, the big school-room, dining-room and wash-rooms; on its first floor were the main dormitories and Matron's room, while the third floor, formerly the servants' sleeping quarters, now provided small bedrooms in which some of the senior boys slept three to a room.

On one side of this central block was the 'private part' of the establishment—drawing-room and headmaster's study on the ground floor; bedrooms for the Sconers, Parker, Mollie Westerly and the spare room, occupied by Carolus on the first floor. There was no second floor.

On the other side of the main block was a bungalow in

which were bedrooms for the staff and the staff common-room.

On the ground floor were ways through to all three parts of the building. One could start in Mrs. Sconer's drawing-room, pass through the private hall to the central block and through this to the staff bungalow without going out of doors. One could also pass from the private part of the boys' dormitories on the first floor.

That Parker had his room in the private part of the house was another privilege that had come with long service. He had made it into something of a bed-sitting-room.

When Carolus returned from the Windmill that evening and was making for his room. Parker opened his door.

"Like a nightcap?" he asked.

Carolus accepted and found that Parker had whisky and a siphon. Parker was a long way from being drunk but he could not have been described as cold sober.

"Been down to the Windmill?" he asked.

Carolus said—"Yes. Strolled across."

"I used to go most evenings," said Parker. "But I find the walk back rather too much for me these days and beer doesn't agree with me as it did."

"How's the rheumatism?" asked Carolus.

Parker looked surprised.

"Oh that! Quite gone, thanks. I don't suppose it was rheumatism. Or just a twinge. Yes, as I was saying I find that just one nip of Scotch at bed-time suits me. This is my twenty-first year with Sconer, you know."

"So I've heard. It's a long time."

"Big part of a life, really. I've seen the school grow from almost nothing. We had eight boys when I first came."

"And now you're sixty-eight."

"Yes. We've worked hard, mind you. Sconer's the best of men to work for. Mrs. Sconer is not such a dragon as some people think. Matron's the trouble there. I'm afraid she's a mischief-maker."

"Pity. I've been hearing tonight about a very attractive member of the staff you had last term—Sally O'Maverick."

Parker looked up.

"What did you hear about her?"

"Nothing really, except that she was very popular and that her dismissal was due to Matron."

"I suppose Pocket told you that? You shouldn't listen to a lot of talk. If it comes to that, Mollie Westerly is thought by most people to be far more attractive."

"She's certainly not the sort of person I expected to meet on a school staff."

"Not at all. She's more . . . more dignified than Sally O'Maverick was." Parker's voice dropped. "Her room's next door," he explained. "She went to bed about half an hour ago. The walls are thin here and I shouldn't like her to think we were talking about her."

"You always have a mistress for the junior boys?"

"Yes. Sconer believes in that. They have more patience with the little ones. We've had a lot since the school opened."

They fell silent for a while. Then Carolus, whose hearing was remarkably sharp, pulled a piece of paper towards him and wrote on it—"Someone is listening at the door." Parker read this, nodded and went on in an even voice—"A lot of masters, too. They come and go. I shouldn't like to think how many."

Listening, Carolus heard from the passage a series of faint taps but they were not on the door of Parker's room. They seemed to waken no response and continued, gentle but persistent.

"Someone's knocking on Mollie Westerly's door," whispered Parker.

The two men continued to sit still and listen. Presently they heard the door of the next room opened and there was a sound of whispering. 'All right, wait a minute', they heard Mollie say impatiently. There was another silent pause, a louder whisper of 'Thank you!' and the door was shut.

With surprising energy Parker crossed the room and threw open the door.

"What on earth are *you* doing here?" Carolus heard him ask. Then, "Come in and explain yourself."

It was Duckmore. He was wearing a dressing-gown and bedroom slippers and seemed to be trembling. He kept his closed hand in front of him as though it held treasure.

"I couldn't sleep," he said. "Mollie told me about the sleeping tablets she brought back from Beirut. I came to ask her for one."

He opened his hand and showed a tiny yellow pill.

"You came right over from the bungalow for that?" asked Parker.

Duckmore's hand was unsteady.

"Yes. They're wonderful. I've had them before. Just one gives you a beautiful long deep sleep, and they seem to work at once—within a few minutes. Can I have a little water to take it with?"

Parker, seemingly perfectly calm, poured some water into a tumbler.

"It's difficult to believe," he said. "Such a tiny little pill. Thank God I don't need anything like that. You'd better get back to bed before it begins to act."

"It's the strain," said Duckmore with a note of hysteria in his voice.

He left them, moving a little uncertainly to the door. They heard his footsteps in the passage as he shuffled away.

"Nervous type, poor Duckmore," said Parker. "He seems

to feel the disturbances here more than anyone. I can't think why. He has private money—quite a lot. I believe. If he's worried about life at St. Asprey's all he has to do is to leave."

"What is his story?" asked Carolus.

"No one seems to know. He was in the last war, I believe. Sconer engaged him about two years ago. He was recommended by the parents of one of the boys. He's a nice enough chap. Perhaps his trouble is that he's studying too hard."

"Oh. He's studying?"

"Yes. Theology. I think he wants to take Orders."

Carolus rose.

"Thanks for the drink," he said. "I must get some sleep."

On the following afternoon when Carolus had spent a somewhat fruitless and irritating morning with Sime's classes, he drove over to Pyedown-Abdale church. He was not surprised to find it a building of some grandeur with a high square tower at the West end, for he knew how many Gloucestershire villages had lost their population and importance and kept only a large church to remind them of the past. The door, on the South side, was open and he entered to find the nave cool, musty and empty. But the door leading to the tower staircase was locked, and without hesitation Carolus drove to the Rectory and asked for Mr. Spancock.

Mr. Spancock nodded vigorously when Carolus explained what he wanted. Carolus was fascinated by his profile, two almost straight lines, one from the tip of his nose to the top of his forehead, the other from the same point to his Adam's Apple, neither chin nor brow breaking the symmetry.

"I'll come with you," he said.

"Please don't bother." Carolus wanted half an hour alone in the tower which had been the scene of Sime's accident.

"Certainly. Delighted. Just let me get my torch. Ah, here we are!" Then with coy slanginess— "Let's go!"

As they approached the door the Rector said— "I'll show you how to get in, any time you want. To the church, that is. Tower's always open—except for the last few days. Police orders. There! See that niche? Key there. Everyone in the parish knows that. Organist comes. Parker, you know. And Skippett—sexton."

They entered the church.

"Fine tower," the Rector said as they approached it. "Been kept locked lately. Police. But they've finished now."

"You mean the police wanted it locked after the accident?"

"Rather! Spent hours there. Photographs. Finger prints. Told me it can be opened now. For bell-ringers."

As the Rector was inserting a large key in the door to the tower Carolus looked up at the vaulted roof above him.

"What height from the ground is the floor of the belfry?" he asked.

"More than thirty feet. Spiral staircase. Worn steps. Death-trap."

They started to ascend and Carolus saw what he meant. He had rarely climbed such a precipitous staircase and the stone steps were as Mr. Spancock said, worn. Each had an indentation of several inches at the centre. If as Sime claimed he had been pushed from the top it was hard to see how he had survived the fall.

The Rector was waving his torch as he led the way and it made shadows and streaks of light on the stone walls. Carolus waited till they had reached the loft in which the

69

bell-ropes hung, then, before more than glancing about him, said—"May I borrow your torch for a moment?"

"Natch," said the Rector smiling at his own comparatively up-to-date utterance.

Carolus behaved rather unexpectedly with the torch, which was large and powerful. He switched it on and kept it on while he returned to the staircase and descended some fifteen steps. Then he began to ascend again playing the torch on the walls to right and left of him at a foot or two only above the level of the stairs. After some moments at about six steps from the top he stooped to examine a small green stain on the stonework on his right. Then he looked at the wall on his left and found opposite to this a similar green stain. Finally he joined the Rector in the loft.

There was not much light here but Carolus could see the bell-ropes hooked back to the wall and on the side of the room farthest away from the top of the staircase an oak table. He made a careful examination of this.

"Rather fine," he pronounced after a few moments.

"Really? Refectory?"

"Old," said Carolus catching the spirit of brevity from the Rector.

Near the top of the stairs were some curtains of dusty red plush some eighteen inches from the wall on which were some rusty hooks.

"Bell-ringers' coats," explained the Rector.

"Ah yes. Does anyone else come up here?"

"Been some trouble before the accident. Seen it myself. Man with field glasses on the tower. Suppose it was Sime."

"Can we go up?"

"Sure!" said the Rector, smiling again. "Follow me!"

They ascended by a ladder permanently fixed to the wall and the Rector opened a trap door. He led the way to leads, moving with noticeable agility. The view was magnificent and stretched in every direction, though St. Asprey's, on the hill, cut off a more distant horizon.

"I don't wonder someone came up here with field-glasses," said Carolus. "This is superb."

The Rector vigorously shook his head.

"Wasn't that," he said.

"No? What makes you so sure?"

"Sime was no landscape lover. Espionage more likely."

"I see. Yes, with a pair of field-glasses one could keep pretty close observation on the school—perhaps recognize everyone moving about. I can see that flashy blazer of Mayring's now. He's on the cricket field."

They started to climb down.

"Awfully good of you to come. Rector," said Carolus. "I'm most grateful to you."

"Seen all you want?" asked the Rector pleasantly as they reached ground level.

"I think so."

"Good. Splendid. Shan't lock this again. Bell-ringers. You must have a look at the glass."

They went up to the chancel.

"No wonder Parker likes playing the organ," said Carolus when he saw it.

"Yes. A beaut, isn't it?" said the Rector. "Choir stalls are fab, too."

They walked slowly down the nave and into the open air.

"I'll run you back," said Carolus.

"Thanks. Don't mind walking a bit. No distance."

"I wouldn't dream of letting you."

"Oh well," said the Rector and climbed in.

When they reached the Rectory and the car was in the drive, Mr. Spancock spoke nervously.

"Can't ask you in, I'm afraid." Then, as though to explain everything, "My wife," he added.

What did one say? wondered Carolus.

"Very sorry. Hope you understand."

"Of course. Thank you again," said Carolus.

(It was some time before he had a chance of asking Mr. Pocket the explanation of this but he found it was a simple one. "She drinks," said Pocket without elaboration.)

It was past half-past four and time to return to the school if he wanted to be there for common-room tea, an occasion usually for conversation, if not confidences.

He drove slowly and some five hundred yards away from the school gates stopped altogether for Duckmore, wild-eyed and obviously out of control, was running full pelt towards him. He quickly jumped from the car and seized the little man as he tried to pass.

"What's the matter with you?" he demanded.

Duckmore stared without recognizing him.

"I'm going," he said. "I must go!"

"Why?"

"There's been an accident."

"Get into the car and pull yourself together."

"No, no! I must go. Sime's dead."

Carolus almost picked the man up and shoved him forcibly into the seat of his car.

"Calm down," he said. "You didn't kill him, did you?"

"No, but . . . I want to get away."

"You shall," said Carolus, driving on to the school. "But not yet. Don't try it that way, Duckmore."

In the drive was Mayring who had apparently come out in pursuit of Duckmore.

"Look after him," said Carolus quickly. "Don't let him try to leave."

The young man nodded and Carolus left them there and

hurried to the staff entrance. Standing at Sime's door was Jim Stanley in the attitude of a guardian.

"You can't go in," he said. "There has been an accident."

"Out of the way," said Carolus, all his normal suavity gone.

"Mr. Sconer says. . ."

This was one of the few occasions on which unarmed combat served its turn. He threw Stanley to the floor three yards away and entered.

The window was wide open and Carolus had a glimpse of green and gold and a peaceful early evening. But facing it, still propped up on his pillows, Sime glared sightlessly ahead, and his chest and the sheets around his abdomen were scarlet with blood. (There was a macabre suggestion of a red pullover as Carolus first looked.) The cause of this was immediately obvious. A long arrow which Carolus recognized as a broadhead had entered his throat just above the adam's apple and remained there falling downward but still deeply embedded. Sime was dead.

But there was another thing which Carolus saw as quickly. On the wall above Sime's head was a large framed photograph of some team, a dozen faces staring manfully at the camera as athletes do. Among them, Carolus had noticed on his previous visit, was the young Sime, no more prepossessing in appearance than Sime at forty, and inexperienced rather than innocent in appearance. This photograph had been shattered by a blow it seemed and some of the chips of glass had showered on Sime's unconscious head.

Carolus looked from the window across to the point from which the archers practised, then made a close examination of the man and the room. He touched nothing.

He was interrupted by Stanley.

"You've got no *right* in here! I was told to keep everyone out till the police come."

"That's all right," said Carolus calmly. "I've seen all I want."

"You had no right. . ."

"Come on. We'll leave this to the police. They have been sent for?"

"I suppose so. Sconer went to phone them."

"Sorry I had to be violent, Stanley. Please accept my apology. I think you will understand later why I had to do it. You're not hurt?"

"No. But I might have been. However, if you come out now I shan't say anything."

Carolus left him standing outside the door again and looked in the common-room. Four cups of tea had been poured out but Parker's was the only one drunk. He looked utterly dejected.

"It will ruin the school," he said.

"Probably. The point is surely that a man's been killed."

"I knew he'd do no good here as soon as he came. What are the parents going to say?"

Carolus seemed about to speak sharply but instead walked out and shut the door.

In the passage he met Sconer with two obvious plain clothes men on their way to Sime's room. Sconer ignored him and he passed the policemen and went to the private part of the house. Without hesitation he entered the drawing-room and found Mrs. Sconer alone there.

"You've heard?" she asked.

"Yes. The police are there now."

She jerked back her head with a pained gesture.

"The police!" she said. "Was it necessary to call them?"

"Of course it was."

"A terrible, terrible accident," said Mrs. Sconer.

74

Carolus lost patience.

"Accident my foot," he said. "The man's been murdered and you must know it."

"Oh no, no!" cried Mrs. Sconer. Then in the words and almost the tone which Parker had used she added, "It will ruin the school!"

Chapter Seven

After that outburst Mrs. Sconer was silent for a few moments then became more practical.

"You have experience of this sort of thing," she said in a somewhat hostile way. "What do you advise us to do?"

"There's not much you can do. The police will investigate and make an arrest. I shouldn't think it will take them long."

"An arrest?" said Mrs. Sconer in a hollow voice. "Here? At St. Asprey's? You mean you think someone connected with the school will be suspected of killing this man?"

"It's difficult to see how any stranger can have killed him."

"Mr. Deene! You came here to help us. I should have thought you would be the first person to say this was an accident. A stray arrow."

Carolus smiled grimly.

"Arrows don't stray into a man's adam's apple," he said. "Sime was killed with remarkable accuracy."

"It *couldn't* have been by chance?" pleaded Mrs. Sconer.

"Virtually, not. At least I can't name a figure high enough for the chances against. It would be several hundred millions to one, I should imagine. I think you will face it all the better when you recognize that Sime was murdered."

"But how can you possibly say it was by someone connected with the school?"

"I said it was difficult to see it any other way. But it is not impossible, of course."

"I hope you may find that. Some passing stranger."

Again Carolus had to suppress a smile.

"But even that would not help the vital question of the school's reputation," went on Mrs. Sconer. "Do you think that any preparatory school can survive a murder?"

"Some of them have survived a good deal. Epidemics, lunacy, fatal accidents, inefficiency, poisoned food, drunken masters and misbehaviour of most kinds."

"You mean this is only a step further?" said Mrs. Sconer optimistically.

"Rather a long step. But I think if the thing doesn't reveal too much scandal you might pull through."

"Must the parents be told?"

"They will read about it in the morning papers tomorrow. It's just the sort of job to appeal to the popular press. Do the names of any of your parents make good gossip column news?"

"Many, I fear. Many. The Minister for Horticulture. Lydia Stripp the film star. The Sheik of Alcalaquiv'r. General Smiling. The Dean of Bournmouth. . ."

"Yes, yes. It's very awkward."

"Do you think we should send the boys home?"

"How much do they know already?"

"Impossible to say. I have not spoken to anyone yet except my husband. But I should say, unfortunately, that the news will have reached them by this time. Perhaps in an exaggerated form."

"It's not the sort of question in which I can possibly be of much use. I can only promise you to do everything I can to get at the truth."

Mrs. Sconer did not seem enthusiastic about this.

"I hope you will find it came from outside." she said dismally.

"What time is it believed to have happened?"

"Please don't question *me* about it, Mr. Deene," said Mrs. Sconer haughtily.

Carolus ignored that.

"When did you hear?" he asked.

"We were having tea. In here. Young Mayring suddenly entered. I was about to remind him that this was the private part of the house when I saw that he was staring and stuttering like a half-wit. 'There's been an accident,' he said. 'Sime . . . I think he's dead.' My husband went with him from the room, and some time later returned to tell me what had happened."

"You saw no one else till I came in?"

"My husband particularly asked me to remain here. I have seen no one. Perhaps Matron can give you more information."

"I'm sure she can," said Carolus and left the room.

Matron could, and was eager to do so.

"I saw this coming," she said to Carolus.

"You. . ."

"Well, it had to come, really. That archery ought to have been stopped from the start."

Carolus looked at Matron's lean face without any affection at all.

"Could you tell me," he asked patiently, "where everybody was this afternoon?"

"I don't know how you expect me to know that," said Matron. "I've scarcely been out of this room. I did happen to see young Mayring going up to the cricket field with the boys. Then Duckmore walked up there by the quick way. But Mayring was back on the archery lawn at four o'clock."

"What about Stanley?"

"He was there too, but I don't know for how long. I noticed him not long before they all came in. He doesn't take the interest some of them do in the archery."

"Do you know where Mrs. Sconer was this afternoon?"

"Mrs. Sconer? She was here for a little while after lunch. There were several things she wished to see me about."

"And after that?"

"I have no idea," said Matron, annoyed at being found deficient. "She may have been in the rose garden. She often goes there in the afternoon."

"But you didn't see her?"

"How could I, from here? The rose garden's on the other side of the house."

"Visible from the other wing?"

"Yes. I can't see everything from here. But I know Mr. Sconer did something unusual for him. He went and had a chat with them on the archery lawn."

"You are sure of that?"

"Of course I am. It was most unusual. He always goes to his study on Thursday afternoons Writing to Parents, till he joins Mrs. Sconer for tea at half past four. He's not a man to break his habits. When I saw him I was surprised. I should have heard anyway."

"You mean?"

"One of the boys would have told me. Or Mrs. Skippett. She was Doing the hall this afternoon."

"I see. Who else was on the archery lawn?"

"They were all there. Mr. and Mrs. Ferris. Mr. Kneller. Duckmore. Mollie Westerly. Quite a party, it was. I was wondering who was supposed to be on duty. Somebody ought to have been supervising the boys' tea."

"No one was?"

"I went down myself when I heard the noise. They came into the dining-room at a quarter past four. After I had been there ten minutes Duckmore came in. I intended to tell Mrs. Sconer of that. It doesn't do for the Men to come late on duty?"

"Where was Parker all this time?"

Matron looked somewhat ferocious.

"I'm sorry to say Parker has developed some very intemperate habits lately," she said. "He came in here for a few moments after lunch while I was giving out medicines. I don't know what he wanted—an aspirin I suppose. He often takes one. At any rate he was at the medicine cupboard. Then he went to his room—it couldn't have been more than half-past one—and I could guess what he went there for."

"What?"

"Well, I knew he had a bottle of whisky there. It went down by more than two inches this afternoon."

"How do you know?"

"I happened to notice. He must have been drinking fast because it was all between half-past one and four because he wouldn't miss his tea."

"What else did you happen to notice, Matron?"

Quite unconscious of irony, Matron continued with gusto.

"There was Something between Mr. and Mrs. Ferris," she said. "Mrs. Sconer doesn't really like them spending so much time at the school with this archery they're so keen on. They *are* parents, after all, and you never know where you are with them. But this afternoon I couldn't help seeing there was something going on between them."

"Such as?"

"She kept walking away and coming back as though they were arguing and she was threatening to leave. Of course I couldn't hear what they were saying but sometimes actions speak louder than words. They went off together, though. Not long after four that must have been. Of course they only live a mile away so they can pop over in a minute in that car of theirs. I used to think it was something else that brought them over, before all this archery started."

"You did?"

"Well, yes, because I couldn't help noticing it when she and Sime were together. That was when Mr. Ferris didn't come of course. I felt I should tell Mrs. Sconer what I'd seen."

"What had you seen, Matron?"

"Nothing, really. Only it was what went on behind the scenes. You can always tell. As if Sime wasn't doing enough mischief, with Mollie Westerly running after him. I don't say it had gone very far, mind you. but I couldn't miss seeing how they looked at one another. That made it awkward, of course. One of the boys' mothers with one of the Men. Mrs. Sconer was quite worried about it long before all this happened."

"You don't think Bill Ferris knew?"

"That's another thing. Just lately I've begun to think he did. Only from what I couldn't help seeing when the archery was going on, but I must say I had begun to think there was more in it than met the eye. You could tell by the way he behaved. I said to Mrs. Sconer, I'm afraid Mr. Ferris has begun to Wonder. She didn't like the sound of it at all, their being parents and everything. But she couldn't get Mr. Sconer to get rid of Sime, for all that. It seems he was very clever with the teaching but as I said to Mrs. Sconer, what's the good of that if he's going to Cause Trouble? And of course as it's turned out I was right. The boys are already talking about this murder and before long we shall have parents coming down to take them away."

"Had anything happened earlier in the afternoon?" asked Carolus relentlessly keeping Matron to the point.

"It depends what you call anything happening. Two of the boys had sneaked away from the cricket field to hang round Sime's window but they must have found him asleep because they were off again at once."

"What time was that?"

"It couldn't have been later than three, and I know it was after quarter to, because the programme I listen to ends at 2.45 and I'd switched it off."

"You don't have a television set?"

"I haven't time for that," said Matron understandably. "I like just the old-fashioned radio because I can listen while I'm doing something else. Anyway, as I say, I had just switched this programme off and was having a few minutes quiet. I happened to be looking out of the window when I thought I heard someone in the passage here. I might have gone to see, if it hadn't been that just then I saw these boys creeping through the trees from the cricket field and thinking that no one noticed them." There was a touch of scorn in Matron's voice for the boys who had so underrated her powers of observation. "It was young Chavanne and a boy called Lipscomb. I guessed where they were going when I saw them dodging about before making for the back of the staff bungalow. But they couldn't have been there a minute. I can't see Sime's window from here, of course, but not two minutes later they were rushing back to the cricket field. I should have told Mrs. Sconer about it if All This hadn't happened. She doesn't like the boys hanging about Sime's window at all hours of the day. Anyway this time they didn't stop there to talk."

"I wonder why not."

"I've thought about that," said Matron. "It must have been either that they saw he was asleep or that his curtains were drawn. He asks one of the Men to draw his curtains sometimes if they go in during the afternoon, so that he can get some sleep."

"Perhaps Sime himself sent the boys away?"

"I hadn't thought of that," said Matron regretfully. "But then again it might have been Mr. Stanley who saw them and sent them back to the cricket field, because *he* won't put up with all that. There was Trouble about the other day, as I told Mrs. Sconer. But whatever it was the boys didn't say."

"Did you see much of the archery itself?"

"I don't take a lot of interest in it," said Matron, "but I couldn't help noticing the way they were doing it this afternoon, as though it was a match or a competition or something. There would be five of them shooting at the same time because they've got five targets."

"Can you see all five archers from here when they're shooting?"

"Well, no I can only see the three," said Matron, evidently speaking with profound regret. "But I can tell if there are five of them out there because of the arrows."

"How many of them were there altogether this afternoon?"

"I can't say that they were all there at the same time, mind you, because the Ferrises went off earlier than the rest and Mayring and Duckmore were up at the cricket field until just at the last. But there must have been . . . well, let's see . . . there were Mr. and Mrs. Ferris, Duckmore,

Mr. Kneller, Mr. Stanley, Mayring and Mollie Westerly. That's seven."

"So they couldn't all shoot at the same time?"

"No. Only the five of them. There was generally one or two waiting for the chance to follow them."

"When they had finished shooting did they go down to recover their arrows?"

"They always do that. All five of them together."

"Leaving their bows behind?"

"That's it. You could see them from here counting up their scores this afternoon. Quite seriously they seemed to be taking it. Some of them went on till quite half past four. The tea in the common-room must have been cold."

"Did you notice if Duckmore remained out there to the end?"

"No, he didn't. I thought afterwards it was funny him being late coming on duty in the dining-room when he wasn't out there the last time I looked. According to what I couldn't help noticing he must have gone in at about ten or a quarter past four, which was only right because he was meant to be on duty for tea at four-fifteen."

"But he wasn't."

"No. As I say, I could tell by the noise that no one was on so I went down. Presently Duckmore came in. I could see he was fussed. I thought at the time it was because he was late on duty but now I wonder."

Did you speak to him?"

"Yes. I did. I felt it was only right because I meant to tell Mrs. Sconer that he was late coming on duty. I said, 'You're very late, Mr. Duckmore'. I thought at first he wasn't going to answer. Some of the Men can be very rude when I speak to them. Duckmore looked at me as though he was trying to understand what I had said. 'Late?' he said, staring like an idiot which I'm really more than half inclined to think him. 'Late?' Then he began gaping at his watch as though he was trying to tell the time and couldn't. I didn't think much of it at the time, except just to remember to tell Mrs. Sconer, but it seems rather funny now, doesn't it?"

"Curious, yes. Did you happen to see any more of him?"

Matron gave Carolus a freezing look. She was put out at him for doubting her thoroughness.

"I came up here after the boys had finished their tea," she said. "There are several who come for their medicine after tea. I always have trouble with the little Fitzsmith because his mother insists on his taking enormous capsules which he can scarcely swallow. They're made of stuff like rice paper and full of some dark crystals inside. It's his doctor at home who makes them up for him. But this afternoon I knew he'd thrown one away because there ought to have been four, one left for that day and three for the next after which I should count out the next week's supply. Little Fitzsmith was so tiresome about it and swore he'd never thrown one away, and I was telling him I should have to tell Mrs. Sconer when I happened to look out of the window and saw something you ought to know."

"Yes?" said Carolus almost breathlessly.

"The front door slammed and out rushed Duckmore looking as though all the furies were after him. I called out, 'Mr. Duckmore! Where are you going?' but he didn't take a bit of notice. I thought I had better go down and tell Mrs. Sconer at once about this, because I knew he ought to be on duty. Of course, I didn't know Anything Had Happened then; it was just that I knew Mrs. Sconer wouldn't like one of the Men rushing out like that and leaving the boys. In the hall I met Mr. Sconer and Mayring. I thought there was something wrong by the look on their faces. I don't usually have much to say to Mr. Sconer but this time I told

85

him that Duckmore had just run out of the front gates like a madman, and he sent Mayring after him."

"Did you then return to your room?"

"Yes. Mr. Sconer went off towards the boys' part of the house and I didn't like to disturb Mrs. Sconer in the drawing-room."

"You were back at your window in time to see me drive in?"

"Yes. I did happen to notice your car and Duckmore getting out of it. I heard you tell Mayring not to let Duckmore get away but I still didn't know what was wrong."

"Really? It was a quarter to five when I picked up Duckmore."

"Yes," said Matron angrily. "It only shows how they were trying to keep it from anyone, doesn't it? You can't tell me some of them hadn't known for some time by then. But was I told? Not till one of the boys came running in and said 'Old Sime's been shot in the eye by an arrow like King Harold at the Battle of Hastings'. Can you imagine it?"

"Which boy was that?"

"Lipscomb. I asked him whatever he was talking about and he said Chavanne had told him. It was All Over the School in a moment."

Carolus did not show the least sign of impatience. Although he was desperately anxious to see the assistant masters before the police examined them, he knew enough of witnesses to realize that in Matron he had the observer of all time. Keen, watchful, malicious, there was nothing she would have missed. She might never again be so informative. With the police she would try to cover up things she thought to the school's disadvantage and even with Carolus, if he returned to question her after her first excitement was over, she might be reserved and difficult. She did not exaggerate for she was too accustomed to having the facts she gave to Mrs. Sconer disputed by erring Men or the boys themselves to take any risks.

"So you did go down to Sime's room?" asked Carolus.

"Yes. But it was too late. There is no key in the lock—I told Mrs. Sconer long ago it Doesn't Do for the Men to be able to lock their doors—but Mr. Stanley was there and Mr. Sconer had told him not to allow anyone in. So I haven't seen It yet. I suppose the police will take It away now?"

"They'll have a lot of photography and measurement to do first," predicted Carolus. "Did Sime's bed always face the window like that?"

"No. It was against the wall on your right as you go in."

"Who moved it?"

"He wanted it moved himself when he knew he had to Lie Up for some time. I suppose he wanted to be able to look out and talk to the boys at the window when they came to see him."

"Did you have it moved?"

Matron hesitated a moment as though wondering whether she was committing herself.

"In the end, I did. When he first asked me I told him it would be bad for his eyes, reading against the light like that. But he kept on about it and said he'd rather be able to see out than be able to read. So I got two of the Men to move it."

"Which were they?"

"Oh I can't remember now. Two of them, anyway."

"Was Stanley one?"

"Was he? Yes, I believe he was, and Mayring was the other. I just asked the two of them from the common-room to do it."

"Was it usual for Sime to sleep in the afternoon?"

"I didn't go down there more than necessary so I don't

know everything. But I think he had a nap after his lunch unless the boys kept him awake."

Reviewing in his mind Matron's pieces of narrative and answers to his questions, Carolus noticed a singular thing. Not once had she speculated on the identity of Sime's murderer, or asked Carolus any questions which suggested the least curiosity about it. In view of her inquisitive nature. there could only be one explanation for that. She knew, or believed she knew, who had killed Sime.

Chapter Eight

Carolus went from Matron's room to the Common Room to find Mayring and Duckmore sitting there in uncomfortable silence. Mayring had evidently taken literally the instruction Carolus had given him not to let Duckmore leave because he sat on a high chair between him and the door while Duckmore was slumped on a settee with broken springs beside the fireplace.

"Have the police been here?" asked Carolus.

"No. They've left a man in Sime's room and gone. I suppose they're with Sconer," said Mayring in a solemn voice.

Looking at the young man Carolus could see that he was scared. This told him nothing for Mayring was scarcely nineteen years old and less than two hours ago had discovered the body of a murdered man. Whatever he knew of this, or even if he knew nothing at all except the fact, one could expect him to be unnerved. Duckmore did not look up when Carolus came in.

"I think I ought to tell you both that I came here at

Sconer's invitation to find out what was causing the trouble. I have a good bit of experience in finding out things. Now I want to get at the truth about Sime's death and I'd like to ask you a few questions."

Mayring nodded solemnly but Duckmore did not stir.

"You found the body, didn't you, Mayring?"

"Yes. I took in Sime's tea as I usually do, and there it was. . ."

"What time was that? You don't know exactly by any chance do you? Don't say anything if you don't."

"I can be pretty exact. The tea is supposed to be put in here by one of the chars at four-thirty. When I came in from archery and found it wasn't here I was pretty annoyed. We'd had a bit of trouble about this tea. On the days when Mrs. Skippett brings it it's sometimes late and once it was already cold when we got it. So I looked at my watch to see how late she was and found it only just after half-past four. At that moment Mrs. Skippett appeared with the tray and Sime's was the first cup poured. So by the time I had put some bread and butter and jam on a plate and taken it in it was, say twenty-five to five. No later."

"I see. Who poured it out?"

"Parker. He usually does."

"Who else was here?"

"Only Stanley. Duckmore was on duty in the boys' dining-room."

"When you saw Sime was dead what did you do with the cup you were carrying?"

"I . . . suppose I must have brought it back here. Yes, I did! I remember seeing it afterwards on the table. I didn't realize what I was doing."

"Do you remember what you said?"

"Not the exact words. I was badly shaken, I can tell you. I said Sime was dead."

90

"How did you know that? You had a cup of tea in one hand and a plate in the other, presumably, so you couldn't very well touch him unless you put them down there."

"How did I know?" repeated Mayring a little wildly. "I could see. Anyone could. His eyes were popping out. There was masses of blood. It was ghastly."

"Yes. I saw it."

"Anyway Parker and Stanley went in at once. They touched him I suppose. Parker told me to go and tell Sconer he was dead and I went."

"Did you go back to Sime's room with Sconer?"

"No. As we came through the hall Matron came hurrying downstairs, flushed up and excited. She told Sconer that Duckmore had run out of the front gates and he sent me after him. Then I met you and that's all I know."

"Is it, Mayring?"

The young man looked confused and resentful.

"Yes," he said. "If I knew any more I'd tell you."

"You'll probably have to tell the police a good bit more than that. About the archery this afternoon, who was there at what times. Perhaps other things which I'm not going to ask you now. Have you discovered who killed your puppy?"

Mayring blinked and hesitated, then said—"Not for certain."

"Whom do you suspect?"

"I don't know. But it's rather strange that when Sime became laid up all those things finished. I didn't jump to any conclusions, of course."

"No. I shouldn't."

Mayring stood up.

"If there's nothing else you want to ask me I'll be running along," he said.

"There is. But it's something you may find difficult to

91

answer. Would you close your eyes a moment? That's it. Now try to see Sime's room as it was when you went in with his tea. Can you see it?"

"I can see him all right. Nothing else."

"Is he in bright light?"

"Oh yes. He is. Was, I mean. Too Bright."

"Daylight?"

"Yes, of course. He was right opposite the window."

"The curtains were drawn back?"

"Certainly. Must have been. His curtains are green things, fairly thick. If they were drawn over and the light was on I should have noticed. It was bright daylight."

"And the window?"

"I'm sure it was open. He kept it open the whole time even when the curtains were drawn."

"Thanks," said Carolus. "There's nothing else I want to ask you just now."

Mayring, looking relieved went out leaving Carolus with Duckmore.

"Cigarette?" suggested Carolus.

Duckmore shook his head.

"What made you run out like that?" asked Carolus gently."

Still Duckmore did not speak.

"You must have had a reason."

"I don't know." The words were muttered rather than spoken.

Carolus pressed on, still speaking in a friendly almost tender way.

"You knew Sime was dead?"

"Yes."

"How?"

Now Duckmore looked up and stared at Carolus in a bewildered way.

"How did you know? You had been on duty in the boys' dining-room. Sime's death wasn't discovered by Mayring until after half-past four. How did you know?"

There was silence in the shabby little common-room, a long silence which Carolus did nothing to break. Then suddenly Duckmore stood up and turning to Carolus looked full in his eyes before asking a most extraordinary question.

"Did I do it?"

Carolus made no answer to that at all, but after a moment or two said in a calm businesslike voice: "Tell me about you and Sime."

Duckmore was seized with almost hysterical loquacity.

"It has been going on all this term," he said. "During the holidays Sime found out something. At least I'd told him, really. He wanted money. He knew I was that most unfortunate person, a schoolmaster with private means."

Carolus, to whom the term could be held to apply, smiled. "There's one person more unfortunate, surely," he said. "A schoolmaster without private means. But go on."

"You see, for three years I was out of the world."

"You mean?"

"In a mental home. Oh, I was a voluntary patient, of course. But Sime knew this. . ."

"How?"

"One day last term I just mentioned the village in which it was: Buckfield in Somersetshire. I said nothing about Holly House, the name of the home itself. Just mentioned the glass in the church there. But when Sime came back this term he had been there and knew the whole story."

"Did that matter?"

"Yes. You see I am studying for the Church. I have always wanted to take Orders. I went to see the Bishop of Bungay—a very go-ahead man. He advised me to do a year or two as a schoolmaster and if all went well he would

93

ordain me. So I knew that if anything went wrong here all my plans would be upset."

"I don't see how Sime knowing that you had been in a mental home could do you much harm. You could leave this school and go to another."

"That's what I thought until all those mysterious things began to happen. If anyone knew about my past I should be suspected at once, as Sime pointed out. It was a terrible position.

"And the only way out of it was to get rid of Sime. That's why . . . I *could* have done it, you know. I was out there this afternoon practising archery with the rest. I know what an arrow can do. I had even felt an urge to do it. I had fought against that, but while Sime lived there was no peace for me—no hope, even. I felt something in me pressing me on to kill Sime. . ."

"With a bow and arrow?"

"When you shoot an arrow at a target you know you are using a lethal weapon. You know that your arrow could kill a man. I couldn't help having thoughts of that kind about Sime. Then when I knew. . ."

"Knew what?"

"Knew that he had been killed. . ."

"How did you know that, Duckmore? You were on duty in the dining-room when Mayring found him. Did you come back to this part of the house after the boys' tea and before you rushed out into the road?"

"I don't know."

"Oh come now, Duckmore, I think you know that. Did you remain with the boys?"

"Yes. Yes. I was in the big schoolroom. Something was hammering in my head. I wanted to get away."

"Yes, but why? *Did you know Sime was dead?*"

"I must have, mustn't I? I told you when I met you so

I must have. That's why I started to run away. I knew I should be blamed. . ."

"But *how* did you know he was dead?" insisted Carolus.

He was watching Duckmore's face and saw a strange expression on it. He looked suddenly shifty, cunning, or was it just hunted? An ugly expression in any case.

"I suppose I must have seen him," he said at last in a resigned voice. "Must have. No one could have told me."

"Only one man knew and that was the murderer."

"I must have seen him. Gone to his room and looked in."

Carolus spoke in a cold and hostile voice.

"Whatever your mental condition, Duckmore, you know perfectly well what were your movements this afternoon."

"I don't! I don't even know whether I did it!"

Unimpressed, apparently, Carolus continued his relentless questioning.

"But when you came on duty late, at nearly half past four, you knew Sime was dead. Had you seen his body or not?"

"Yes. I had. I came in from the archery range and went to the common-room. I was due to be on duty at four-fifteen and it must have been that then. I thought I'd just take a peep at Sime to see if he wanted anything. I looked in and saw what had happened. So I ran to my room."

"Why didn't you give the alarm?"

"You don't understand. After all I've been through these months, with Sime telling me I should be thought guilty of everything, I was terrified. I wished I hadn't seen it. For ten minutes at least I fought to pull myself together."

"Did you go back to the common-room?"

"No."

"Was there anyone there when you left it before going to Sime's room?"

"No one. I didn't see anyone at all. I just stayed in my room for ten minutes trying to get myself in a condition to go on duty. At last I felt I could do so and went through to the boys' dining-room. But I was late and they'd nearly finished tea. Matron was there and mentioned that I was late. All the time the boys were at tea and in the big school-room afterwards I was trying to decide what to do. I knew I should be suspected of killing Sime. It was too much for me and I made a bolt for it."

"Didn't you realize that 'making a bolt for it' was the worst possible thing for you in the circumstances? That in the minds of most people it would condemn you out of hand?"

Duckmore seemed more alert now and looked at Carolus shrewdly.

"I didn't realize anything," he said. "I felt a hammering in my head and *had* to get away."

"You were on the cricket field this afternoon?"

"Yes. For a while."

"Then you went to the archery range?"

"Yes. For half an hour."

"And from there direct to the common-room?"

"That's it. So far as I know. But I would like to be certain, you know. I don't remember. . ."

Carolus looked at him calmly.

"It will all come back to you," he said.

They were interrupted by the entrance of one of the plain clothes men whom Carolus had seen earlier.

"Which is Mr. Duckmore?" he asked.

Duckmore rose. His face was quite expressionless now.

"We'd like to ask you a few questions," said the police-man coolly and without showing even that false and slightly patronizing respectfulness, that repetitive use of the word 'sir', which is the normal police manner of approach. Duckmore went out with him.

Carolus lit a cheroot and smoked it thoughtfully. The

case interested him. He found it difficult to feel deep sympathy for any of the people involved. The Sconers were not an amiable couple and their concern seemed wholly for the school in which they had admittedly invested their money, time and energies but which did not seem to Carolus of outstanding importance in the scheme of things. Sime seemed to have been a highly unpleasant individual if Duckmore's story was true, while all Carolus knew of Matron conformed with his experience of schools of this kind, a sour and intriguing woman, a power behind the throne and in the opinion of all 'the Men', including probably Sconer himself, a malicious bitch. Of Mollie Westerly he had formed no sort of opinion and Mayring was not, he felt, quite the likeable young public school man he wanted to seem. Parker, after twenty years of this life, was (understandably perhaps) 'taking to drink' while Bill and Stella Ferris had something ostentatious and *faux rustique* about them. Stanley, as a favourite of Mrs. Sconer and Matron, was at a disadvantage and might not be a bad fellow while Kneller was deep and as yet inscrutable. Any one of these, Carolus felt, who had the opportunity *might* have killed Sime, and that was what gave the case its intrinsic interest. But there were unknown quantities here, too. Had anyone else been on the premises that afternoon? What about Horlick, the gardener? And more insistently, why had Sime kept a loaded pistol in his room? Where was it now? And why, within a few moments of knowing Carolus, had Sime entrusted him with a letter to 'Mrs. Ricks' which he did not want others to see? The murder itself did not seem to him quite such a problem as some of the corollary questions.

Young Mayring returned.

"There's something I think I ought to tell you," he said. "I couldn't say anything in front of Duckmore."

97

"Well?"

"It was something that happened after you left me with him. We came here together and were sitting quietly when suddenly he came over to me and, looking quite barmy, said: 'I did it'. I couldn't believe it for a moment and made him repeat it. Then with an awful sort of grin he said—'I, said the sparrow, with my bow and arrow, I killed Cock Robin'. I told him not to be an ass. It shook me, I can tell you."

'Yes, I suppose it would."

"When he said that about the sparrow it was like some awful joke, but the first time, when he said 'I did it' it sounded as though it was true. If he did do it it must have been by a tremendous bit of luck because he's not much of a shot."

"Who *is*?" asked Carolus who did not seem much impressed by Mayring's story.

"Jim Stanley, I should say," said Mayring quickly and rather sulkily, and did not seem inclined to talk any more about archery.

Chapter Nine

The boys, startled but chattering, were somehow got up to their dormitories where they assailed Matron with questions when she made her rounds.

"Please Matron, is it true Mr. Sime has been murdered?" "Matron, what do we do if the murderer comes here and tries to strangle Pumfret Minor?" "Do the police know who did it?" "Have you been questioned, Matron?"

"Now stop talking rubbish, boys," said Matron crisply. "There has been a little accident. Nothing for anyone to get excited about. You'll all be in trouble with Mr. Sconer if you don't go to sleep at once."

"Please, Matron, I can't go to sleep while there's a murderer about."

"Silence! It's time your light was out. Into bed, Paxton."

When Matron switched off the light there were cries of alarm, mostly feigned, and very soon afterwards the silence was complete but for a few awed whispers.

Meanwhile the Men were gathering for staff dinner which

would be a lugubrious affair that evening. Usually Mrs. Sconer, in a dress which emphasized her dignity rather than her figure, smiled graciously to Stanley who sat on her right and condescended to Jumbo Parker on her left, while Mr. Sconer, though he looked up nervously to his wife from time to time, found courage to talk to Mollie Westerly who sat beside him, or even to Matron who, with her thin neck protruding from her dark green dress looked like a stem of *arum maculatum*, the wild plant we call lords-and-ladies, sat on his left. Between these two trios sat usually only Duckmore and Mayring but now Carolus had joined them.

A moment's embarrassment was caused to everyone that evening by Jumbo Parker who appeared in a dark suit usually reserved for Sunday Church and known to be his only outfit beyond the sports coat and flannel trousers he wore everyday.

"Mrs. Sconer Won't Be Down," announced Matron solemnly when they had taken their places.

The meal was eaten almost in silence except when Matron ventured to explain her difficulty in getting the boys to sleep to which none of the Men added the customary comments on the little abominations, the intolerable ruffians and so on, which usually followed anyone's complaints about Boy in general.

Towards the end of the meal Sconer had a surprise for them. Speaking for the first time since they had sat down he said—"I should like All You Men to come to my study after dinner. There are one or two things we must Go Over."

There were mutterings of assent and Matron looked, as Mayring remarked afterwards, as though she were feeling seasick.

"Will you want me, Mr. Sconer?" she asked loudly.

"Won't be necessary thanks, Matron. Just a few little

100

things I want to go over," repeated Mr. Sconer firmly. He grew almost dignified when his wife was not present. "Shan't need to bother you either, Miss Westerly," he added.

The Men gathered with that assumed casualness which among Englishmen betokens at least concern, perhaps tension. Parker pulled at his large pipe and everyone knew that he allowed himself only two pipefuls of tobacco a day; Duckmore and Mayring smoked cigarettes. Stanley did not smoke. They waited till Sconer asked them to sit down and Carolus thought there was more curiosity on their faces than anything else.

"I've asked you Men to come here," said Sconer, "because we must Go Over one or two things."

There was a long pause. Then, to the mild surprise of Carolus, Sconer made no direct reference to the murder, expressed no regret for the death of Sime and showed what seemed to be his sole concern.

"If the school is to survive," he said, "we must all make a concerted effort. Mrs. Sconer and I have been considering the matter and feel that with the future of the school in danger we should appeal to you to do everything you can to . . . make a concerted effort. . ."

A curious cacophony of low grunts came from the Men.

"In the light of what has happened we did at first consider asking the parents to take the boys home for the rest of the term, but we decided this would be most unwise. But something must be done to show that we are conscious of the gravity of the situation so we have decided to *cancel the school sports.* I am sending a letter to the parents tomorrow explaining that after the unfortunate accident of this afternoon we feel it would be inappropriate to hold them. I have also said that from today no form of . . .

101

archery will be practised on the school premises or by any of the staff. I have asked Kneller to see that all the paraphernalia of this pastime should be immediately removed. I wish I had done so long ago."

The grunts this time were in a lower key.

"The police," said Mr. Sconer, "seem convinced, unfortunately, that Sime . . . that the accident . . . that there has been . . . what is the word I want?"

"Murder," said Carolus.

"The police," began Sconer again, ignoring this gaffe, "are not wholly satisfied that the . . . incident was due entirely to carelessness. But I can see no reason at present to think that the newspapers . . . We can only hope that nothing sensational will appear."

"What about the inquest?" asked Stanley.

"I am coming to that. It would be most unfortunate, *most* unfortunate, if it was suggested that Sime's er . . . death was anything but accidental. I have seen Kneller about this and he assures me that such accidents have been known among the practicants of this very foolish and reprehensible er . . . sport. I trust that any of you who may be called as witnesses will bear him out on this. The school might survive a fatal accident but any suggestion of deliberate action would quite destroy the confidence of the parents."

"You'll never get away with it," said Carolus.

Sconer flushed.

"I should be grateful. . ." he began.

"No coroner's jury in the world could possibly be persuaded to call it an accident. Sime's room was *behind* the line from which the archers were shooting."

"We know all that," said Sconer angrily. "What you fail to see, Mr. Deene, is something far more decisive. That is, that there could be no possible motive. I have not your experience in these matters but I *do* know that to convince any reasonable person—and jurymen are surely responsible —that anything like a murder has been committed, you must be able to suggest a motive. What *possible* motive could there have been here? Sime was a most popular man."

Carolus smiled.

"Have it your own way," he said. "I should have thought your chances would be better if you faced up to the truth. After all, it wasn't one of the boys who was murdered."

"No, but if we are to accept your monstrous premise the parents would feel that they may be in danger. If we admit the possibility that among us there is one capable of conniving at the death of a colleague we might as well close the school at once."

Carolus said no more and the meeting broke up into groups. Before they dispersed however they had promised Sconer all the support they could give. Personal hostilities and jealousies, even the grey eminence of Matron seemed to be forgotten and earnestness was the keynote of their assurances to Sconer.

"Tomorrow," said Sconer optimistically, "I want the school to go on as though nothing had happened. We don't want morbid ideas to spread among the boys."

As the Oldest Member, Parker made a suggestion.

"I think if the boys know that Sports Day is cancelled it will leave them nothing to talk about but what happened this afternoon. Why not let them go on practising and have the sports without parents?"

"And have them writing home about sports to which their parents haven't been invited? No, no, Mr. Parker. But it might be advisable to give them something to take their minds off . . . Something immediate. Has anyone any suggestion?"

Mayring blushed and said, "Why not a school play?"

"Ye . . . es," said Sconer a little dubiously. "Nothing realistic, of course."

"In the open air! Scenes from *A Midsummer Night's Dream*!" went on Mayring, losing his head somewhat.

"There would be no harm in their rehearsing, anyway. It would keep them interested. Yes, start tomorrow, Mayring. Work in as many of them as you can."

"What about the costumes?" asked Mayring tactlessly.

"That can all be gone into later. Now. . ."

"Chavanne will make a marvellous Titania!" said Mayring, completely carried away.

"Yes. Yes. You see to all that," said Sconer impatiently.

"Would Matron help with the costumes?" suggested Mayring, who seemed to have lost all hold on reality.

"No doubt. Now there are more urgent matters to discuss. What about the match against St. Cartier's tomorrow?"

"It would be a pity to scratch it," said Stanley. "Young Lipscomb's in cracking form."

"So he may be, but I feel it will Look Bad if we play as though nothing had happened. What do you think Mr. Parker?"

"I don't know anything about it," said Parker huffily. "You may remember you suggested that I should give up coaching the cricket team three years ago, when Sime came."

"We can't go into all that now," retorted Sconer. "The thing is, must we scratch the match against St. Cartier's?"

"No!" said Stanley. "Let's play it out."

"Very well. The boys must be told not to talk to the other team at tea-time. Well, I think that's all."

"I was thinking about the play," said Mayring. "Do you think I ought to play Duke Theseus?"

"I think. . ." began Sconer, then seemed to repent of the

guessable retort he was about to make. "Do as you think best, Mayring," he said.

When they dispersed Carolus walked away quickly, unwilling to hear any more that night. Though all of them had seen the dead body, the blood, the distended eyes, he seemed to be the only one to whom this meant the horror of a stolen life. He could never take murder lightly, believing that the murderer usurped the attributes of God, but nor was he influenced by sentimental or emotional considerations. The murder of a man like Sime, clearly a cad and perhaps a crook, was no less murder than the killing of an innocent child. though it might move one less to indignation and pity. The people with whom he had been tonight seemed far more concerned with their school and its reputation than with the dreadful thing that had been done.

He slept fitfully and came down to breakfast without his usual sense of renewed energy. He felt himself watched by the small boys at his table and guessed they were nerving themselves to ask questions. He decided to forestall this.

"Why did you and Lipscomb sneak away from the cricket field yesterday afternoon?" he asked Chavanne.

"We didn't really sneak away," said Chavanne.

"Did you ask permission?"

"I was going to ask Mr. Mayring only he was bowling to that ass Whitlock."

"You haven't told me why you came."

"It was only to see Mr. Sime, sir. He said we might come and look in at his window. Only when we got near we found the curtains were drawn across and Mr. Sime said if the curtains were drawn we were never to disturb him."

"You didn't look in?"

"No honestly we didn't, did we, Lipscomb? We could see the curtains were across before we got there so we turned back and scooted like billy-o."

"I see. I don't suppose you know what time this was?"

"Oh yes, I do. I know exactly what time it was. I know to the very second what time it was. I know. . ."

"All right. Don't keep on about it."

"It's an extraordinary thing how I know though, sir."

"How do you know and what time was it?"

"I know absolutely exactly because we got up to cricket at two o'clock and Mr. Mayring said he'd bowl to me and Lipscomb at the nets because we're playing St. Cartier's Away on Saturday and we ought to have some practice because they've got a beastly fast bowler. . ."

"Yes. Yes. The time?"

"Well Mr. Mayring said he'd give us twenty minutes each and start with Lipscomb because he's easily our best bat only he can't bowl and Mr. Mayring said he was going to give him some jolly fast leg breaks and Lipscomb said not *too* fast. Mr. Mayring looked at his watch and by the time he started bowling to Lipscomb it was ten past two so he went on till half past and then I went in. Mr. Mayring's a jolly good bowler. I think he's easily the best bowler in Gloucestershire. . ."

"How long did he bowl to you?"

"He timed it exactly and gave me the same as Lipscomb. Twenty minutes. It didn't seem long while I was batting. That ass Whitlock was waiting to go in after me only Mr. Mayring told him to hang on a couple of minutes. Then he started bowling to him. So me and Lipscomb did a bunk to see Mr. Sime, so I know exactly what time it was—five to three. Must have been, mustn't it, sir? Does that tell you what time Mr. Sime was murdered?"

"Eat your breakfast and don't talk nonsense."

"Bet he was murdered, though. Bet I know who did it."

"Bet you don't. Bet *I* do," said Lipscomb.

"That's quite enough thanks," said Carolus.

"Bet it was old Spancock," said Chavanne.

"What did you say?"

"The Rector, sir. I know he was here that afternoon because I saw his rotten old car. Only he didn't leave it in the drive in front of the house where the parents leave their cars but in the lane by the cricket field. I saw it there when we went up to the cricket field at two o'clock. But it wasn't there when we scooted down to see Mr. Sime."

"Who do the police suspect, sir?" asked Lipscomb excitedly but Carolus was saved giving pompous and meaningless reproofs by the end of breakfast.

The morning passed uneventfully. Whatever the police may have been doing in Sime's room or elsewhere, the boys were kept to routine and efforts were made to prevent them from seeing or hearing anything unusual. In the break Mayring announced his forthcoming production of scenes from *A Midsummer Night's Dream* to one or two senior boys and within minutes the news had travelled to the lowest reaches of the first form where piping voices said—"Are you going to act, Miss Westerly?"

After lunch, having with great tact arranged with Parker to accept a bottle of whisky in return for taking Carolus's duty on the cricket field and at tea, Carolus drove away, conscious of Matron's observation from the lattice of her bower.

A few moments later he reached the churchyard and passing through the lych-gate stood quite still on the flagstone path which ran to the church doors.

There were three yew trees in the churchyard, fine old specimens of the tree which in past centuries was planted in burial-places because as an evergreen it symbolized immortality. These trees engaged Carolus's attention and when he had looked into the church and found it empty he

107

began to search among the lower branches of one of them as though he were birds-nesting. He spent some fifteen minutes in this way, then went on to the next tree. After a few minutes he found what he was looking for. A branch had been recently hacked off.

Carolus examined this carefully and as he did so was aware that someone was approaching from behind him. Turning, he saw the Rector.

"Hullo. Snooping again?" said Mr. Spancock cheerily. "You seem to find the church interesting."

"I do. It has a fine tower," said Carolus. "Who looks after the churchyard?"

"Oh, Skippett," said the Rector.

"I beg your pardon?"

"The sexton. Skippett. One of my parishioners. Wife works at the school."

Carolus remembered the little woman he had met on the first day.

"Oh yes. Does he look after things pretty well?"

"Yes. Yes. Splendid. Conscientious. Thorough."

"He lives in the village, I suppose?"

"Number 8, Council Cottages."

"Thank you."

"Terrible about Sime," said the Rector and Carolus saw that he was watching him keenly.

"Yes," he replied without comment.

"Accident?"

"No, murder."

"Impossible. Can't be. Unbelievable."

"You knew him well?"

"Casually. Not well. Seemed a nice chap."

"When did you see him last, Mr. Spancock?"

"I? See Sime? No idea."

"Had you been to the school yesterday afternoon before

you were kind enough to come over to the church with me?"

"The school? Hardly. Called on Mrs. Kneller. Blind, you know. Why?"

"Your car was noticed in the lane by the cricket field."

The Rector smiled.

"Ah yes. Always leave it there when I call on Mrs. Kneller."

"You didn't see Sime?"

"Sime? No."

"I thought perhaps as he was laid up you might have been in to see him."

"Intended to. Should have another day. Wish I had. But no. Mrs. Kneller only."

"Thank you very much."

"Not at all. Delighted. Any information. Shall we see you in church on Sunday?"

"I'm a Catholic," Carolus explained.

"Ah. Romanish Persuasion. Let's hope all these little distinctions will be obliterated soon, eh?" beamed the Rector.

Carolus took his leave.

Chapter Ten

No. 8 Council Cottages turned out to be one of a dozen small and offensively pink villas among the grey Cotswold homes of Pyedown-Abdale. All their doors were painted dark green and there was nothing to distinguish one from another except the chromium digits above their chromium letter-boxes.

Mrs. Skippett opened the door.

"You gave me quite a turn," she observed accusingly to Carolus. Since during his previous conversation with her, she had been given the creeps, the shivers and the shudders, he realized that her reaction to his appearance was a comparatively mild one. "I told you what it would be with that Matron and now you see what's happened. You better come in and not stand gossiping on the doorstep or what will people think? They want something to talk about round here."

Carolus came in to a small sitting-room furnished with the shoddy varnished ply-wood furniture of the day, and

110

hung with nylon curtains while the ornaments, vases, and ash-trays were of plastics in pastel colours. The ugly Euclydean mass-produced carpet, the chairs covered in shining nylons, and process-printed pictures, gave him in turn those symptoms from which Mrs. Skippett suffered, the creeps if not the shudders. Nor did he fail to notice the grey corpse-like face of the television set.

"I'm trying to find out who killed Sime," he began, but got no farther.

"It *is* a problem isn't it? From what I know about it any of them might have done it because there wasn't one of them hadn't their knife into him one way or another till it quite gave you the shakes to hear the way they carried on. That Matron, now, she couldn't bear the man and as for Mrs. Sconer, *well*. Still, there it is, it's done now and you can't say fairer than that."

"There was something I wanted to ask your husband," said Carolus.

"Oh, *him*. Well, he'll be in in a minute and you can ask him what you like. He'll tell you if he can. He's not like these people from round here who're afraid to open their mouths. We don't come from these parts otherwise you might find us like what they are, never so much as stopping for a few words if they meet you in the street and as for enjoying a chat, not them. I always say there's no need for them to be like so many oysters, but no, they won't have it, and Mrs. Horlick who works up at the school's just the same. Anyone might be a waxen image, but there you are. My husband's the opposite. If he knows anything he'll tell you. I often say to him, you can't keep anything to yourself, I say. It was just the same when my auntie was alive."

"He's likely to be in soon?"

"Oh yes. He won't be long. He works in his own time

you see, but I usually know when to expect him. Well, so they've done for that Sime properly this time. D'you know who I think it was?" Mrs. Skippett went on chattily. "I think it was that Duckmore. I've always thought there was something funny about him. The way he looks at you and that. It gives me the jumps when I see him. Here's my husband coming now."

Mr. Skippett was not much taller than his wife and almost as garrulous. He had a narrow bald head and wore gold-rimmed spectacles.

"He wants to ask you about the murder," was Mrs. Skippett's greeting, introduction and explanation in one.

"Oh, does he?" said Mr. Skippett with a gold-toothed smile as he shook hands with Carolus. "I can't say I know much about it, to tell the truth. Only what the wife has told me. I never go up to the school if I can help it. Too much tittle tattle up there."

"What I wanted to ask you is nothing directly to do with the school . . ." began Carolus.

"That's a good thing because its right outside my knowledge, what they get up to. I did hear about them putting that rat in the Matron's bed and wondered wherever they got it from. A rat's not a thing you can lay your hand on just when you want it. But when it comes to them murdering one another with bows and arrows, well, I said to the wife, we might be back with Robin Hood."

"You look after the churchyard, don't you, Mr. Skippett?"

"Have done for a good many years. The Rector before this one, Mr. Tomhurst, asked me if I would and I didn't like to say no."

"You remember the Saturday afternoon on which Sime was found at the foot of the tower staircase?"

"I remember it all right, but that's not to say I was up

112

there that afternoon. I went up on the Sunday, twice, as I always do."

"But you wouldn't have spent much time in the churchyard on Sunday."

"No, but I was up there all Monday. I always spend Monday there. Where it is, they throw their cigarette ends away before going into church and empty packets and I don't know what. You wouldn't think people going to church would leave a lot of litter like that but you'd be surprised."

"So you tidied up the churchyard that Monday. Did you notice anything unusual?"

Mr. Skippett thought hard and looked disappointed.

"I can't say I did." he said. "Not to say out of the ordinary. There's always a bit to tidy up."

"You didn't find some little branches of yew stripped from a bigger branch?"

Mr. Skippett brightened up.

"It's funny you should say that, because that's just what I did find. Quite a lot of them, there were, pushed into the hedge down in the far corner. I thought at the time, that's funny, but I'd quite forgotten it until you mentioned it. Yes, there was quite a lot of them. I said to myself someone must have wanted the stick for something and cleaned them off."

"I told you he'd be able to tell you," put in Mrs. Skippett proudly. "He's quite a one for noticing things and doesn't mind who he tells about it."

"You've never found the stick from which they were cut, I suppose?" asked Carolus.

"No. That I haven't done. But you wouldn't expect to, would you? Whoever troubled to do that wanted it for something and took it away."

"If he had of done, he'd tell you," said Mrs. Skippett.

113

"He can't keep anything to himself. Same as me. I must come out with it, whatever it is."

"That's good, because there are one or two things I'd like to ask you, Mrs. Skippett. You were working in the hall yesterday afternoon, I believe?"

"Not al the time, I wasn't. But Mrs. Sconer's very particular about the hall and I must say it does look nice when it's done with the parquet, and that. I can't bear to see anything Let Go till you don't know whether it's got polish on or not. Gives me the willies, anything like that. So I was in the hall most of the afternoon."

"Did anyone pass through?"

"I shall have to think," said Mrs. Skippett. "I started there soon after I'd had my dinner in the kitchen. Half past one it may have been. Mr. Parker came downstairs and went off to the boys' part of the school. He was back a few minutes later and went up to his room. I thought, you're going to have a nip at the whisky bottle, I thought. Well, he does like a drop or two now and again, especially lately."

"Then there was Mrs. Sconer coming down from Matron's room, perhaps half an hour later. 'I'm going out to the rose-garden, if anyone wants me,' she said to me, quite pleasant, as she went by. I thought, you've been upstairs hearing the latest from Matron, I thought. But I didn't take much notice, not at the time."

"Did you see either of those again?"

"Not till tea-time. Then Parker came downstairs, after his tea and it reminded me to take it through to the common-room. About the same time Mrs. Sconer came in from the garden."

"Anyone else?"

"Let's see. There was Mr. Sconer came out of his study and went through to the boys' part, or it may have been to the staff part, you can't tell because as you know you can go right through. I thought, someone's going to catch it, I thought. But he wasn't long gone. He came back not more than ten minutes later and went into his study again. I thought, it's a good thing he hasn't got one of the boys with him because you know what that means and I don't like it when he takes the cane to one of them. It gives me the horrors when you hear one of them howling out. But yesterday there was nothing of that."

"Anyone else?" persisted Carolus.

"Yes, there was. This is the funny part, really. Mollie Westerly came down from her room and went through to the boys' part. I thought, I know where you're going. you're going to see Sime. And sure enough not five minutes later Stanley came in and asked me if Miss Westerly was up in her room. I told him, no, she's just gone through to the boys' part and he dashed off as though he were after her. I thought, that'll lead to trouble, I thought. But I didn't see either of them again. Nor anyone else, so far as I can remember. But of course I wasn't there all the time. Mrs. Horlick and I usually have a cup of tea before I take the staff tea to the common-room but she was off yesterday and I had my tea alone. Anyone could have been about in the hall then and I shouldn't have known."

Carolus prepared to leave but without much confidence in being able to do so promptly.

"I'm most grateful to you both," he said.

"That's all right," said Mr. Skippett. "Only too pleased."

"If there's anything else you want to know, don't mind asking," Mrs. Skippett added.

"You're welcome to what little I can tell you. I only hope it puts some idea in your head."

"It's no good asking Mrs. Horlick anything because it was her afternoon off. If you want to know you come to me and I'll tell you what I can."

115

"Same with the church part of it. What I don't know nobody can tell you and I'd be only too willing."

"Well, thank you," said Carolus reaching the door and getting it open.

"It's not as though we had anything to hide," said Mrs. Skippett, following him into the entrance passage. "Not like Some."

"I never was one to want to hush things up," said Skippett as Carolus opened the front door and passed through it.

As he left them on the pavement and made for his car he heard their farewells.

"Don't forget, if you want anything!"

"You just pop in here and I'll tell you!"

Waving politely Carolus drove away.

Back at the school he was approached by Mayring who spoke with the awed relish of a schoolboy sending another to the headmaster's study.

"The police want you," he said. "They've taken over the common-room for their enquiries. They've had me in and kept me nearly an hour. Like Inquisitors!"

Carolus was accustomed to C.I.D. men but was in a weaker position than usual this time, in fact might be himself a suspect. He had heard of the man in charge of this enquiry, a certain Detective Superintendent Osborne, famed for his thoroughness and his overbearing manner. Carolus rather looked forward to the encounter.

He entered the common-room to find the table had been moved and Osborne, with the local man Haggard, was sitting behind it.

Osborne looked up.

"Wait outside, please," he said. "I'm not ready for you yet."

Carolus smiled and decided to bide his time. He went

116

out, and meeting Duckmore asked him where tea was being served for the staff. Hearing it was in Matron's room he went there. Five minutes later a flustered Mayring looked in and said "They want you *now*!"

Even then Carolus did not take any petty advantage of the situation by letting Osborne wait. He finished his tea and went.

Osborne, a heavy man with a big expanse of pale cheeks and a very small mouth, had grey hostile eyes and a harsh voice.

"Your full name, please," he said and Carolus told him.

"Do you know that it is a very serious offence to obstruct the police in the execution of their duties?" asked Osborne.

"Yes, isn't it?" agreed Carolus. "And how often the police themselves are guilty of it. But don't let's waste time with chit-chat, Superintendent. What do you want to know?"

"I warn you, Deene. I know you've been a nuisance in previous cases. You'd better understand that I won't tolerate that sort of nonsense. If you take one false step I shall charge you with obstruction. This is a serious case and I'll have no amateur theatricals disturbing my enquiries. What are you doing here, anyway?"

"Teaching," smiled Carolus. "So far only small boys. I hope I don't have to end by teaching you, either manners or your job. But *do* lets get down to essentials. I detest badinage, don't you?"

"Kindly tell me exactly what you did yesterday afternoon."

"Certainly. That's the sort of question I like," said Carolus, and proceeded with lucidity and precision to describe his movements from lunchtime onwards, while Osborne made notes.

"Why did you go to the church?" interupted Osborne.

"I wanted to take a look at that stairway down which Sime had fallen. Very steep, that stairway."

He went on to describe his return, his meeting with Duckmore, his visit to Sime's room.

"Were the curtains drawn back when you entered?" asked Osborne.

"Yes. There was sunlight on the dead man."

Carolus continued with his story, his interviews with Mrs. Sconer and Matron, his return to the common-room. Osborne studiously refrained from asking any questions about his impressions or conclusions, but enquired on what day Carolus had arrived, how he had come to leave one school for another, when he thought of leaving. In answer to the last Carolus said—"Oh, not *yet*."

"There's nothing more I want to know from you but you'll be required to attend the Inquest. The Coroner may want to know more about your presence here. Meanwhile. kindly refrain from any kind of interference. You may go now. Unless you wish to make any statement."

Was there, Carolus wondered, a gleam of hope or curiosity in the Superintendent's eye? Could it be that after dismissing Carolus's pretensions to insight as 'amateur theatricals' he at least wondered whether Carolus might have anything interesting to say? Carolus looked solemn.

"There is one thing," he said, "which I think deserves consideration."

Osborne had apparently returned to a study of his papers.

"Well?"

"There are Ferrises at the bottom of our garden," said Carolus and had the satisfaction of seeing Osborne's small mouth open wide. He left the room, but when he was chatting with Parker some hours later he agreed with the oldest

118

member of the staff that Osborne was 'no fool, whatever else he might be'.

Mayring was waiting for him when he left the common-room, looking anxiously inquisitive. Once more he reminded Carolus of a boy waiting outside the headmaster's study to hear how many strokes a friend had received.

"What did they ask you about?" he said.

"Oh, this and that," said Carolus.

"They asked me about my dog being killed. How do you think they knew about that?"

"An old bird told them, probably."

"You mean Matron?"

"It might be anyone."

"They knew. They knew all I said about what I would do to whoever had done it. Do you think they suspect me?"

"I've no idea. Osborne is not the chatty sort."

"Of course I would never have said things like that if I had known what was going to happen."

"I'm sure you wouldn't," said Carolus drily. "Did you tell Osborne you suspected Sime of killing your dog?"

Mayring looked startled.

"I didn't suspect him!" he said. "Or not more than anyone else."

"Not even when all the nocturnal disturbances ceased after his accident?"

"I thought it was strange, but I didn't . . . I say, Deene, *you* don't suspect me of killing Sime, do you?"

"I haven't got as far as having suspicions yet. Pity about the archery. I hear you were becoming a very good shot."

Mayring looked like a rabbit being chased from its burrow by a ferret.

119

"Not really," he said. "I often missed the *whole target*!"

"I daresay William Tell did that too when there was no particular inducement to be accurate. Ah well, see you at staff dinner."

Chapter Eleven

Next day was Sunday and Carolus took advantage of this to follow up a clue, hunch, piece of evidence—he scarcely knew what to consider it yet. Mrs. Ricks, 22 Sapperton Road, Cheltenham—the address in Sime's scrawling handwriting on the letter the dead man had asked him to post.

It was a blustery morning when he set out and he found Cheltenham in the throes of Eleven O'Clock Service. The streets were almost empty, the pubs by a piece of legislation magnificently Victorian being closed until mid-day to prevent their licence-holders competing with the clergy for popular patronage. There was a self-satisfied look about the place, he thought, as he went to the address he wanted.

No one answered the bell. No. 22 was a solid house built late in the nineteenth century. The Dombeys might have lived in it. It looked now grim and somewhat neglected but not, Carolus felt, unoccupied whether its inmates were just then at home or not.

He rang again without result and was about to turn away when the door of the adjoining house opened and a tall woman, elderly and inquisitive, looked out. She made some play of seeing Carolus for the first time and said—"Oh! Did you want Mrs. Ricks? She's gone to church. St. Bravington's."

"Thank you."

"Is there anything I can tell her?" asked the tall woman hungrily.

"Not really, thanks."

"She'll be back soon. It's the Vicar preaching this morning. He never keeps them long."

"Good. I'll come back."

"Who shall I tell her called?"

"Oh don't bother, please."

"What's the time now? Ten to? She should be here soon after twelve. Would you like to come in and wait?"

"That's very kind of you."

"I'm on my own this morning," said the tall woman, preceding Carolus into a drawing-room decorated with Victoriana not recently acquired but in its natural state. "I went to Early Service, you see."

"Quite."

"I don't know what Mrs. Ricks will say when she finds I've been entertaining her visitor," she went on with a touch of coyness. "She doesn't approve of me, I fear. I *am* rather unconventional, I suppose!"

"You are?"

"Dear Mrs. Ricks is so *very* correct. Of course, in a way I admire her for it. But I was brought up to *enjoy* life. You have known her long?"

"I don't know her at all, I'm afraid. I have to see her on a matter of business."

"Oh yes. Connected with her niece, perhaps?"

Was it? Carolus wondered.

"She may not care to discuss business on Sunday. She is very strict about Sundays. When her niece was staying with her..."

Carolus made a bold plunge.

"Miss O'Maverick, you mean?"

The tall woman eyed him keenly.

"I only knew her as Sally," she said. "But as I have explained, Mrs. Ricks and I are not intimate friends. I understood that her niece had been a schoolmistress. She came here to convalesce. Such a pretty girl! And a great favourite with the men. You could see that."

Carolus longed to say 'how?' but smiled and waited.

"There had never been so many callers as during the time she stayed with Mrs. Ricks. Rather older men, mostly. But I shouldn't like you to think I was given to gossip."

"Of course not."

"One of them was a schoolmaster, I understood, from the school where she had taught. There was even a negro gentleman. From Birmingham, I believe. Or so Mrs. Bobbins, that's my kind little char, told me. You see she worked for Mrs. Ricks until quite suddenly, a few months ago, just after the niece arrived, Mrs. Ricks told her she didn't need her any more and I jumped at the opportunity. Chars are not easy to come by. Even you as a man must know that. And little Mrs. Bobbins is a treasure."

What was more, an informative treasure, thought Carolus.

"She had ceased to work next door when this negro gentleman came," went on the tall woman, "but she hears of things."

"Indeed?"

"I don't think Mrs. Ricks was very pleased when she started working for me," smiled the tall woman with satisfaction. "Not that she could suspect me of listening to gossip, but well, *you* know."

"I expect she, like everyone else, has things about her she doesn't want known," suggested Carolus.

"She has, and she keeps it locked up in a cupboard," said the tall woman snappishly. "I wish people would be more open. Here we are, two elderly women living next door to one another and you'd think to see us we were complete strangers. I've noticed it more lately, since her niece came to stay. I *do* think people might *share* their confidences and everything else a little more. Don't you? They are funny!"

Again Carolus suppressed the answer he would like to make and instead of 'Hilariously!' said "They are sometimes, yes," quite seriously.

"I have a great sense of humour," went on the tall woman. "I often find myself laughing at nothing at all. When Mrs. Bobbins told me about Mrs. Ricks not speaking to her niece for two days I couldn't help smiling. So petty, to sulk like that."

Carolus had his back to the bay-window which was lace-curtained, but he noticed that the tall woman's eyes kept peering beyond him.

"Here's Mrs. Ricks now!" she said, and they both looked out.

Opening the iron gate was a fur-clad middle-aged woman whose face seemed to express disapproval of the world at large. The eyes were cold grey-blue and the corners of the mouth were turned down. She carried a large prayer-book.

"I should give her time to go upstairs and take her things off," counselled the tall woman. "Otherwise she'll be fidgeting to do so all the time she's talking to you. She's like that. Always wants to do things correctly. Not like me. I'm

124

slapdash, really. Don't let her see you come out of here. She wouldn't like *that*. I hope she's not going to say she won't see you on the Sabbath. I'll keep my fingers crossed for you."

Mrs. Ricks, as she stood in her front doorway and glared at Carolus, seemed about to say more than that. But Carolus got a word in first.

"I'm from St. Asprey's School," he said quickly.

Mrs. Ricks glanced to right and left, chiefly to left, in the direction of the tall woman's bay window.

"Come in!" she said.

If the tall woman's drawing-room was Victorian this was more gloomily so, a stuffy ugly room in which the air had not been changed for weeks. Mrs. Ricks pointed imperiously to a mahogany chair upholstered with black horsehair. The corners of her mouth were so far down that they seemed to wrinkle her chin, "Please state your business," she said.

"It's not as easy as that," said Carolus, only too truthfully.

"Sime is dead, I understand."

"Yes. Murdered."

"Indeed? I'm hardly surprised. But I can't think what it can have to do with me."

"You can't?" said Carolus desperately.

"I certainly can't. I only saw the man once."

"But he wrote to you on the day before he was killed."

There was no change in the severe expression of the face when Mrs. Ricks heard of this but that may have been because the mouth corners could sink no lower.

"On a matter of business."

"Would you allow me to see the letter? I am investigating the circumstances of his death, you see."

"The letter is destroyed."

125

Carolus, becoming fairly sure of his ground, took the offensive.

"Where is your niece now?" he asked.

"I have sent her away. It is not the smallest use your trying to find her. I am determined not to be involved any further."

"Unfortunately there are the facts," said Carolus with admirable ambiguity.

"What facts? My niece stayed with me some weeks. That's all."

"Sime knew a great deal more than that," said Carolus grimly.

"I don't know whether this is an attempt at blackmail or not," said Mrs. Ricks. "If it is I can assure you that it will end in serious consequences for you. I am not the sort of woman for that, as I told Sime. I don't care what he told you. . ."

"He told me nothing. He didn't even discuss it with me."

"Then *why* do you presume to come here?"

"I've come for information, Mrs. Ricks, not money."

"I have no information to give," said Mrs. Ricks sharply, evidently not believing him.

"But you have, you know; information which will help me discover who killed Sime."

"Whoever it was relieved mankind of a scoundrel," said Mrs. Ricks decisively. "I have nothing more to say."

"I'm sorry, but I must ask you certain questions."

"By what possible right? You know perfectly well it is no affair of mine. In my position. . ."

"Your position, Mrs. Ricks, is that you have been an accessory to a serious crime. I'm sorry to have to be so blunt but I must have the information I need."

"How dare you say accessory? The girl is my sister's daughter. I could not turn her out of the house."

"In her condition, no. But you allowed that Birmingham negro. . ."

"Stop!" said Mrs. Ricks dramatically. "What is it you want to know?"

"The most obvious thing first. Who was responsible for her condition?"

"And that," said Mrs. Ricks almost triumphantly, "is the one thing I cannot tell you!"

She glared at Carolus but he thought he saw the corners of the mouth faintly quiver.

"You haven't told me your name," went on Mrs. Ricks more calmly.

Carolus told her, adding that he was only at St. Asprey's to try to clear up the troubles there and did not wish to cause her embarrassment. To his surprise the corners of the mouth went up.

"Mr. Deene," she said, "I am a lifelong believer in temperance. I practically never Touch Anything. But at a moment like this I feel perhaps we both require a little restorative. For purely medicinal purposes I *do* keep securely under lock and key, a small quantity of alcohol." She produced a key. "Perhaps you would kindly go to that cupboard. I scarcely feel well enough to do so myself."

Opening the cupboard in a heavy bureau Carolus found it remarkably well-stocked, indeed he could not remember a better supply of hard liquor in a private house.

"I'll have a Scotch myself," said Mrs. Ricks. "You will? You'll find a siphon in the other cupboard. Thank you." Then in a voice like a sigh of gratitude, "Ah! That's better."

Carolus followed her example.

"You were saying?" said Mrs. Ricks, her mouth now a horizontal straight line.

"I said that I must know who was responsible for your niece's condition."

"I only know it was someone at that school. Nothing would induce my niece to say any more. I tried everything to get the information from her, as you may imagine. It was to no avail. For all I know it may have been Sime himself."

"Sime tried to blackmail you?"

"Yes. Quite unsuccessfully. I never knew how he discovered that my niece was here. It was all most unpleasant. I have a position to maintain. When my niece first told me how matters stood I refused to have anything to do with it. But she has no parents and I feel she is my responsibility. I never condoned the steps she took. The negro you speak of was introduced to the house during a visit of mine to London. But even when she told me what she had done I could not bring myself to abandon her. It has caused me a great deal of anxiety and distress. I need scarcely say that such things were foreign to my experience. I have had a somewhat sheltered life."

"Sime knew of the negro?"

"Yes. He came over here soon after it . . . happened. I had a most disturbing interview with him, but I did not give way. He said the most abominable things. I have never in my life felt so degraded. He even suggested that I might go to prison for complicity, as he called it. When I said that I knew nothing of this man being sent for from Birmingham he said, quite vulgarly, 'Tell that to the Marines.' But I had made up my mind." Those mobile corners of the mouth were not for nothing, Carolus realized. "He didn't get a farthing from me."

"How did you get rid of him?"

"I said I had not got a cheque-book. He replied that he did not want a cheque but what he called hard cash. He then told me he would call on a certain day when he would require £500 in notes. He did not seem in the least afraid that I would inform the police that I was being threatened with blackmail. He knew I had too much to lose. My good name, my position in the town. . ."

The corners sank to their old uncompromising disapproval.

"Did he call on the promised day?"

"No. He sent me a letter instead—the letter you mentioned. He explained that he had had an accident and could not get about. But I should hear from him when he was better. It was very cleverly put because no one reading the letter would guess anything was wrong. You can imagine how disgusted I am with the whole thing. Help yourself and give me just the tiniest drop more."

"Thank you. Say when."

'When' was a long time coming and Mrs. Ricks gave a faint smile as she sipped, the corners now clearly upturned.

"There is another thing I should like to ask you," said Carolus. "Who paid for the gentleman from Birmingham?"

"I hope you know how distasteful it is for me to discuss such matters," said Mrs. Ricks. "The whole thing is thoroughly sordid, like something one only read about in the servants' Sunday paper when I was a girl."

"Yes. I'm sure. Did you pay it?"

The corners sank.

"Certainly not. I did not know anything about it till I returned from London. Fortunately I had taken the precaution of dismissing the Daily Woman I employed at that time. It has meant great inconvenience, but I knew she was given to gossiping and felt it would be wise to be alone with my niece. It's a good thing I did in the circumstances.

I have a next-door neighbour who is grossly inquisitive and I have no doubt she would have learned everything. My niece, in fact, used to say that she reminded her of the School Matron at St. Asprey's who is also given to peeping from behind curtains."

"Not from behind curtains," said Carolus. "Matron, to do her justice, leans right out of the window to get a wider conspectus. But you have not told me who paid this man's charges? They must have been considerable."

"Must they? I know nothing of such things, needless to say. Nor do I know who paid them. My niece had no money of her own. I certainly never questioned her about it. There is a limit to my endurance and the money side of these disgraceful transactions was unthinkably squalid. I don't think you realize the position I occupy here, particularly in the parish of St. Bravington's. Another little tot?"

"Not for me, thank you," said Carolus. "What about you?"

"I don't mind," said Mrs. Ricks. "Just a suspicion. Like last time."

"I am sorry you won't let me see your niece. It means I shall have to find out for myself where she is and go there. You might just as well save me the time and trouble."

The corners went down.

"No. And you won't find her. I don't think you'd gain anything by it if you did. I can probably give you all the information she could."

"Except on that one point. Would you tell me how she spoke of the various people at St. Asprey's? The headmaster, for instance?"

"She rarely mentioned him. I gathered only that he was hen-pecked. I believe she considered him a clever teacher, but of a personal nature nothing emerged. She detested his wife and the Matron and gave lively descriptions of their system of espionage and intrigue."

"What about a master named Stanley?"

"I don't think she cared for him much. At least she once said he was a nonentity. I gathered that he was too much in the confidence of Mrs. Sconer and the Matron. But there was an older master she liked very much—Parker. She used to call him Uncle Jumbo and once described him to me as an old pet. My niece had a very careless way of talking, you see."

"There is another master called Duckmore."

"She was reticent about him. I once wondered whether he might not be the man . . . in question and asked her. She shook her head and said she did not want to talk about Duckmore."

"That leaves only the gentleman cook. Kneller."

"She was more friendly with his wife than with him, I gathered. But she spoke in quite a friendly way of both."

"Did she know some parents called Ferris?"

Mrs. Ricks looked up.

"No," she said. "I don't think so. I certainly never heard her mention them. Why do you ask?"

"They live quite near the school and are frequently there."

"Strange. She must have known them. I thought I had heard of all her acquaintances there. Ferris. Ferris. No. I am sure she never said anything about them. I must ask her . . . when I see her. You did say 'Ferris'? I find that altogether unaccountable."

She's overdoing it. Carolus thought.

"I'll tell you whom she *did* like," went on Mrs. Ricks with corners up. "That was a man named Horlick, the gardener. I grew quite tired of hearing of his virtues. In my position I always feel it's a mistake to encourage people of that sort to be familiar and when my niece began to refer to him by his first name, (it was Gervase I seem to remember) I protested sharply."

Carolus stood up.

"Thank you for all your information, Mrs. Ricks."

"One for the road?" she said incongruously and with corners high.

Carolus refused and left her, corners down again with disappointment in his capacities.

As he turned to put the catch on the cast iron gate he was aware of a tall shadow behind the lace curtains of the house next door.

Back at the school after lunching in Cheltenham and taking a thoughtful drive, Carolus heard several pieces of news. The parents of five boys had removed them but only one father, a writer of detective stories, had been abusive to the Sconers saying that he did not want his son contaminated. Mayring had held a preliminary meeting in the gymnasium to allot parts in his production of *A Midsummer Night's Dream*. There had been a good deal of dispute about these and Chavanne had flatly refused to play Titania, irreverently suggesting that Matron should be asked to do so. Parker had been very upset by the removal of the boys which he saw as a presage of ruin to the school and had disappeared to his room where—Matron said—he had half a bottle of whisky concealed in the Po cupboard beside his bed. Duckmore had been behaving in a most eccentric way, counting the boys like sheep as they walked into the dining-room. Stanley and Mollie Westerly were still on their afternoon walk. Only Matron had remained conscientiously at her post and reported fully to Mrs. Sconer.

Yet Sconer, with whom Carolus chatted before dinner, did not seem unduly perturbed. Perhaps he was hoping that the parents who had called that day would be the only ones to remove their sons. He seemed quite willing to help Carolus in his enquiries and asked about the classes Carolus had taken over from Sime. Carolus found this attitude somewhat puzzling.

Chapter Twelve

Carolus was glad when Parker asked him to come in for a nightcap. There was a simplicity about 'Jumbo' Parker, a lack of the common malice of the place, which he liked. He could talk to Parker where with everyone else, suspects or not, he had to be guarded and watchful.

Not that Parker was very cheerful that evening. The removal of boys from the school had upset him a good deal and he speculated gloomily about the number they would lose after the Inquest. Then, as though he realized that Carolus might not be deeply interested in the fate of St. Asprey's, he said, "And where have you been all day, Deene?"

"Cheltenham," said Carolus. "I went to call on a Mrs. Ricks."

"Who's she?"

"She's the aunt of Sally O'Maverick, the girl you had here as a mistress last term."

134

Parker smiled.

"Charming girl," he said. "We were all a little in love with her. Did you see her?"

"No. She's away. Did you know someone here had put her in the family way?"

Parker looked serious.

"I suspected it," he said. "Was it Sime?'

"I don't know. I was hoping you could tell me. Sally refused to tell even her aunt. With whom was she friendly?"

"She was friendly with everyone—that's the trouble. Even with me, though I own she used to call me 'uncle'. Stanley, Sime, Mayring, Kneller, Duckmore, Horlick the gardener."

"What about Bill Ferris?"

"Yes. She used to go there. But she was friendly with his wife as well—not that *that* means anything nowadays."

"It's a bore," said Carolus. "I hate poking about among people's adulteries and aberrations. But I shall have to find this girl. So much depends on the man's identity."

Parker smoked his pipe and looked puzzled.

"Do you think it does?" he said. "Connected with the murder of Sime? I can't quite see how they are related."

"Sime was trying to blackmail Sally's aunt," explained Carolus. "Someone had paid for an abortionist and Sime knew it."

"I see. He really *was* an abomination, wasn't he? Yes, I can see that you must find Sally. It shouldn't be very difficult, for *you*."

"Or for you. The aunt remembers how kindly Sally spoke of you. Don't you think that if you were to write to her the aunt might forward the letter?"

"I wish you'd find her some other way," said Parker. "That would be rather a breach of confidence on my part, you see. I know you have to do these things when you're

135

looking for a murderer, but if you can leave me out of it I'd be grateful."

"Well, I have got other enquiries to make," said Carolus. "I haven't seen Bill and Stella Ferris yet."

"I wonder why not," said Parker thoughtfully.

"I'll tell you. In a case like this I often find that the information I want most comes to me in interviews which the informants themselves have sought. I have a feeling that several people will speak to me during the next few days."

"The Inquest is on Thursday," said Parker.

"I've never learned much from an Inquest," said Carolus. "Except something of the art of mendacity. Anyway, I hope to have clarified my ideas before then."

The next morning after breakfast Mr. Sconer invited Carolus to his study, and looking about him there Carolus was lost in bitter memories of his own preparatory school. He wondered which arm of which chair supplied the place of execution and which drawer held the dreaded implement.

"Mrs. Sconer and I," said Mr. Sconer giving a precedence which was second nature to him, "feel that we should not take up any more of your valuable time."

"Don't worry about that," said Carolus. "I'm enjoying myself."

"You kindly came here to investigate some mysterious and unpleasant nocturnal events. Unfortunately you were not able to explain them before a greater blow fell. Now we feel that our whole enterprise is in jeopardy, and that we shouldn't detain you longer."

"I'm interested," said Carolus blandly. "I don't at all wish to back out just now."

"Then I must speak more bluntly," said Sconer who could be a bold man when his wife was not present. "You are no longer welcome here, Mr. Deene."

"That's all right," said Carolus. "Almost all the enquiries

136

I have to make are away from the school. In Cheltenham or elsewhere. I'll move down to the Windmill Inn."

"What I meant was, we should like you to cease all enquiries on our behalf."

"I will, certainly. As from now. But I shouldn't think of dropping them on my own behalf. I've told you, I'm interested."

"This is monstrous," said Sconer. "My wife and I invited you here in the first place to make certain investigations. We now wish you to cease them as the police have the whole matter in hand."

"Sorry," said Carolus. "I've set my hands to it, as they say. I shan't be happy till I know who killed Sime and *why*. But as I've told you I don't need to stay at the school for that."

Mr. Sconer seemed dubious as though he had not been briefed for this contingency.

"It's not a matter of your staying at the school," he said. "You are, of course, welcome to stay. It is that I find it . . . with the police. . ."

"I see," said Carolus.

At that moment Mrs. Sconer entered.

"My dear," said her husband. "Mr. Deene says he cannot possibly drop his investigation at this point."

Mrs. Sconer surprised them both.

"I should think not!" she said. "He has not yet discovered the truth and it is *only* the truth that can possibly save the school now."

Mr. Sconer looked as though he doubted this.

"Please continue, Mr. Deene," went on Mrs. Sconer majestically. "I hope you will leave no stone unturned."

"I shall have to be away for a day," said Carolus.

"By all means. My husband will arrange for one of the Men to take your classes."

"I have to trace a piece of information elsewhere."

"We quite understand," said Mrs. Sconer. Her husband seemed about to say something, but caught her eye. Carolus left them to sort it out.

His prediction to Parker that he would be approached by others, with or without information was fulfilled that day with unexpected promptitude, for after lunch Mollie Westerly came up to him.

"Like to take a breather in the garden?" she asked with characteristic directness. "I want a bit of a natter with you."

Carolus saw that in spite of her breezy manner there was a disturbed, perhaps frightened look in her rather fine dark eyes.

'Yes. Let's go. I've heard a lot about the rose-garden."

It was a still warm afternoon and the girl, so unlike a schoolmarm, so nearly beautiful, dressed with elegant discretion, seemed again to Carolus a most unlikely person to find in this scrubby little hotbed of malice and suspicion. Yet she was obviously very much concerned in it.

"I gather you have quite a bit of experience of situations like this," she said rather accusingly.

"Not quite like this," said Carolus. "But I have investigated murders before."

"I know. That's why I want to talk to you. I think I'm in trouble."

"You think you are?"

"Well, yes."

"Surely it's clear-cut. Either you had something to do with Sime's death or you didn't."

"It's not quite as simple as that. Do you think I'm under suspicion?"

"I think we all are."

"You too?"

"Why not? I was here when it happened."

"But you weren't on the archery lawn. But I was. What's more I was shooting from the corner which can't be seen from Matron's window. It's directly in front of Sime's. But that's not all."

Carolus waited. Yes, there was fear in the brown eyes.

"I hated Colin Sime," said Mollie Westerly after a moment. "I suppose because I thought at first I loved him."

"Most people here seem to have hated Sime, except the boys," said Carolus gently.

"They haven't said so. I did."

"Perhaps you should tell me about that."

"Oh yes. I mean to. It was on the day before he . . . his death. You see, during the first weeks of the term I thought . . . well, I went about with him a good deal. I suppose in a way I was attracted to him. He was a man with that peculiar thing people call 'a fascination for women'. No one has ever defined it—all you can say is that some men have it. Well, Sime had. At least for me. But after a time I began to discover what a howling cad he was."

"How?"

"What do you mean 'how'?"

"How did you discover?"

"Oh . . . Everyone knew. No one liked him. I could see it."

"You had no real reason?"

"Reason? No. What's reason got to do with these things?"

Carolus persisted.

"You didn't, for instance, think that he was blackmailing anyone?"

"Blackmailing? No. Was he?"

"He has been accused of it."

"Of course I'm not surprised, but I didn't know that. I just realized he was a rotter and wanted nothing more to do

139

with him. But it's not so easy when you're on the same staff. Besides the awful thing was that he still had a sort of hold on me. I can't explain. He had a very strong personality you know. I couldn't quite get free of him, and I hated him for that. Am I making sense?"

"Admirably. Do go on."

"It wasn't like me. I've always been a pretty decisive kind of person. I think he knew that. He used to jeer at me for it. Yes, Mollie, he used to say, you want to be quit of me, don't you? But you can't, my dear. That sort of thing. It was infuriating."

"Then I . . . well, I suppose I fell in love with Jim Stanley. I don't think you know him very well. He's . . . he has . . . I mean, he's. . ."

"Quite," said Carolus.

"As soon as Sime saw us going about together he was furious. I can't think why because he never really cared for me at all. But he did everything he could to turn me against Jim. And he watched us all the time. You've heard how he used to take the field-glasses from the shooting range up to the top of the tower when we were out for a walk? It was *beastly*."

"Tell me about the day before he was killed."

"I'm coming to that. He sent Mayring to say he wanted to see me and like a fool I went to his room. He began shouting at me. He was in a filthy mood. Presently I lost my temper and I remember saying—'I could kill you, Colin!' My back was to the door when I said it and I turned round to see Matron standing in the doorway. She'd come down for something she said. She'd heard what I said and next day, after Sime had been found dead, she reminded me of it. 'Pity you said that', she told me. 'Anyone might think you meant it'. I'm sure she has told the police."

140

"If the police suspected all the people who said they could kill Sime, or words to that effect, it would be a long list. If they suspect you it must be for some other reason."

Mollie stopped.

"What other reason?" she asked.

"I have no idea. When did you last see Sime?"

"Then!" said Mollie a little excitedly. "That afternoon when I told him I could kill him. The day before he was murdered. I never saw him after that."

"You didn't see him later that afternoon?"

Mollie stared at him. She seemed about to say something, but fell silent.

"I may be mistaken," he said. "But I thought that just after tea that afternoon I heard him say 'Hullo, Mollie', to someone who had knocked at his door and gone in."

"Yes. You're right. I didn't mean to mention it because it was so sickening. I went to say I was sorry. You know, he had a sort of horrible hold on me."

"I'm glad you told me that," said Carolus. "What about the next day? The day of the murder?"

"I never went near him, thank God! That I'll swear to. I stayed in my room after lunch, then, soon after three, went out to the archery lawn."

"Which way did you go?"

"Downstairs in the private part, through the hall into the big schoolroom and out. I didn't enter the staff bungalow at all."

"When did you see Stanley?"

"Jim? He came to the archery lawn soon after I got there. Why?"

"He didn't follow you to the staff part of the house?"

"No. He'd have told me if he had. Why do you ask these questions?"

141

"I like to follow everyone's movements that afternoon. He went to look for you in the private part of the house just after you came through the hall from your room. He asked Mrs. Skippett if she'd seen you."

"It all sounds so important now, doesn't it?" said Mollie sadly. "Such trivial things do. Yet all that might have happened any afternoon."

"Murder's like that."

"Do you think I'm suspected, Mr. Deene? Tell me frankly."

"Not on what you've told me this afternoon," said Carolus..

Was there a touch of exaggeration in Mollie's relief? "*That's* all right, then," she said.

When Carolus reached the common-room it was empty, but after a while Mayring came in wearing his spotless flannels.

"Left my pipe here," he explained looking round for a large cherry-wood incinerator which he was learning to handle.

"How are the rehearsals going?" asked Carolus.

"Terrific. Lipscomb's going to be terrific as Bottom and I've decided to play Oberon myself—the king of the fairies, you know. Chavanne's Puck. It'll be absolutely terrific."

"I hope you don't lose any of your cast after the Inquest."

"There is that," said Mayring soberly.

"I've got one question for you, by the way."

"Oh Lord! I want to get up to the nets. You know we lost to St. Cartier's on Saturday. . ."

"I won't keep you a moment. Did you go into Sime's room just after lunch on the day of the murder?"

"What makes you ask?" fenced Mayring.

"Curiosity. Somebody must have. You were here in the common-room weren't you?"

"Yes. I was. I can't remember whether I went into Sime's room then. I certainly found him later."

"I know about that. Did you go in just after lunch?"

"I may have. I often do."

"I wonder why you are so evasive. You will certainly be asked this at the Inquest."

"I'm not evasive. I can't remember everything."

"You say you often went to his room after lunch. Any particular reason?"

"Oh he was laid up. Couldn't move. I went in to see if he wanted anything."

"And did he? That afternoon?"

"No. Jumbo Parker was in there, having a chat. He's about the only other person in the place who would speak to Sime."

"Except Mollie Westerly."

"I suppose. But not if she could help it."

"But you got on quite well with Sime?"

"Yes. I was sorry for him when he was laid up. Rotten luck, in the summer term. Now I *do* want to get up to the cricket field."

"Were the curtains in Sime's room drawn when you left?"

At that moment Jumbo Parker came into the room.

"I can't possibly remember," said Mayring. "You had better ask Parker."

Carolus did.

"Mayring tells me that you were chatting with Sime when he looked in after lunch on Friday. Do you happen to remember if his curtains were drawn then?"

"No. They can't have been because I drew them for him. He asked me to because he wanted a nap."

"What time would that have been?"

"Somewhere between half past one and two," said Parker. "I don't know exactly."

143

"Well, now I *am* going to cricket," said Mayring.

As he opened the door a chorus rose from those waiting in the passage.

"Please sir, may I play Quince?"

"Please sir, Chavanne says if he's got to wear a goblin hat he doesn't want to play Puck. May I play it, sir?"

"Please sir, Matron says we can't use pillows for Bottom's padding."

"Shut up!" shouted Mayring desperately, "and get up to the cricket field, you mooncalves."

Chapter Thirteen

When he went outside he found Kneller waiting for him. Yet another of these information volunteers he thought. But Kneller in his deep abstracted way—though he obviously had something to communicate—was not in a hurry to come to the point. He asked Carolus what he thought were the chances of the school's being able to continue, not disguising that his chief anxiety was to retain possession of his cottage.

"When this was a private estate," he explained, "my wife's father was the agent here and she was brought up in the cottage in which we live. She could never feel as sure of herself anywhere else. I hope you will come across and see us sometime. My wife would be delighted. She likes meeting people."

Carolus said he would certainly do so.

"She does not get many callers," said Kneller. "The Rector occaisionally. D'you know Spancock?"

"Yes. He seems quite a lively character."

"Very abrupt, though. I can scarcely follow him."

"He was at your cottage on the afternoon of Sime's death, I believe?"

"Yes. He dropped in unexpectedly not long after lunch. He wanted to hear about Sime. He was up at the church at the time of the accident, you know."

"Then why didn't he go to see Sime?"

"They didn't Get On," said Kneller. "There was some trouble once when Sime criticized Parker as an organist. All very trivial, I expect, but the Rector preferred to ask us for news of him. He didn't stay ten minutes."

"He didn't go in for archery then?"

"He came out one afternoon and had a shot but couldn't get an arrow on the target. By the way, the police have taken all my archery equipment, I suppose for examination. It's a bit of a bore but as Sconer has banned archery for this term it doesn't matter so much. I can't see what they'll get from finger printing that stuff. Everyone has handled everything."

"Did you keep an exact tally of the arrows you had?"

"Yes. We've lost several since we've been practising. But Sime wasn't shot with one of those we use on the targets, you know."

"He wasn't?"

"No. It was a hunting arrow or broadhead. I showed you one of them before."

"I remember. A fearsome thing. The shaft was rather longer I seem to remember. Could you screw an ordinary arrow's shaft on to the hunting arrow head?"

"No. The thread is different."

"But you might be able to shoot one broadhead among the target arrows without being noticed?"

"Easily, I should think. When we're practising each of us is chiefly concerned with his own bow and arrows and target, of course. He wouldn't be looking round at the next

146

man's. Of course when they all walked down to the targets it might be noticed."

"The arrow which killed Sime was one of yours, of course?"

"Yes. At least I presume so. One of my broadheads was missing."

"When did you discover that?"

"Not till after the murder, unfortunately. They were kept apart from the others. When I heard that Sime had been shot with a broadhead I went and checked and found one missing. Someone must have been pretty confident of himself to take only one for a job like that. Suppose he had missed?"

"Suppose William Tell had missed," said Carolus facetiously. "What a lot of words and music it would have saved us. Schiller's too much for me, anyway."

"But I like Rossini's music," admitted Kneller. "Anyway, Tell did hit the apple and whoever killed Sime did. . ." A slow and rather ugly smile appeared on Kneller's face . . . "hit the adam's apple," he finished.

Carolus became more businesslike.

"Had everyone easy access to all the arrows at any time?" he asked.

"Good gracious, no. You don't think I would leave them unlocked with fifty little fiends of boys about, do you? The summer-house where they were kept had a strong lock with an enormous key and I locked up after we had finished practising each day."

"But while you were all here it was open of course. Were the arrows you weren't using, the broadheads for instance, in a locked box?"

"No. I see what you're getting at. Any of us could have extracted a broadhead without being noticed, probably."

"That's what I wanted to know."

They were interrupted by Stanley who strolled up so casually that Carolus guessed he had some purpose in joining them.

"I hope you two chaps realize you're being watched," said Stanley.

"From Matron's window, you mean? When are we ever *not* watched from there?"

"She can't see the rose garden, though," said Stanley with satisfaction. "She doesn't know that you and Mollie had a natter this afternoon."

"Don't be too sure of that." Kneller sounded damping. "It's not only observation with Matron. It's her information service."

He nodded grimly and without another word walked away in the direction of his cottage.

"Strange chap, Kneller," said Stanley inevitably and banally.

"Think so? He seems to know a lot about archery. He has been telling me about the different kind of arrows. Sime was killed with a broadhead, apparently."

"Was he?" said Stanley with marked indifference. "What am I expected to do about it? Weep?"

"It was murder," said Carolus.

"Of course it was. How else could Sime die? It's a wonder it didn't happen years ago. People like that can't shuffle off this mortal coil unhurriedly. Someone's bound to do for them."

"You make no secret of your feelings."

"Why should I? I didn't kill him—though it surprises me I didn't. No one can possibly suspect me."

"I can't quite see why not."

"Me? When everyone knew how I felt about the man? When I'd said a dozen times that I'd like to strangle him. *Would* I be such a fool?"

148

"On that I have no opinion. What had you against Sime? Apart from the congenital loathing you felt for him about which you are so frank."

Stanley sounded very contemptuous.

"Only that he was trying to get possession of the school —that's all."

"How do you know that?"

"Believe it or not, he actually told some of the boys that he would be headmaster next term. He also said something of the sort to me during one of our rows. How this was to come about he did not say. But he seemed quite sure of it. I don't know how he proposed to get rid of the Sconers. Or perhaps he saw himself as their partner. He had it all planned out, anyway. You may be sure that if anything of that sort ever did happen the first change he would make would be to sack Kneller and me. But I did not take the threat seriously."

"Did anyone?"

"I don't know. I shouldn't think so. Oh, by the way, Stella Ferris asked me to ask you if you'd come to their place for cocktails this evening. About six. She says they've scarcely met you yet."

"Yes. I'd like to."

"Perhaps you'll give Mollie and me a lift then? We can show you the way."

So at six o'clock Carolus drove to the pretentious entrance of a large Cotswold house built about eighty years ago in the style of an earlier century. The garden was well-kept, but given to statuary and artificial pools rather than flowers, and the door was opened by a butler or at least an individual dressed as one; perhaps a survival or perhaps an impersonation, Carolus thought.

The hall was rather grand but lacked mammalia or any sign of taxidermy because Bill Ferris was (unexpectedly in

149

such a hearty good mixer,) anti blood sports. The house smelt of expensive cigar smoke, expensive flowers, expensive scent.

"Mr. and Mrs. Ferris are in the library," said the character who had opened the door in a suitably bass voice as he showed them the way.

The library was a charming room, given its name, presumably, because there was a small book-case near the window containing modern novels. Carolus managed to sit beside this and saw, as he expected, all the right names—Murdoch, Snow, Braine, Sillitoe, Waugh, Greene, but under them, with a more used look about them, Christie, Allingham, Queen, Blake and other writers of crime novels.

Bill Ferris opened a drink cabinet and began to handle its utensils with an air which suggested an exhibition of cocktail mixing.

"The usual, darling?" he said in his rich plummy voice to his wife.

"*Need* you ask?" returned Stella, without much good humour, Carolus thought.

"My wife always has a Bronx," Bill explained to Carolus after pouring, shaking and pouring in a deft and practised manner. "I expect you'd rather have a dry Martini?"

"Thanks. I'd like a Scotch and soda, please," said Carolus dampingly.

"*Not* a cocktail man?" said Bill. "You're right, of course. They're Out at the moment except the old Dry Martini. But we like them."

"Darling, don't talk such nonsense," said Stella in a tired irritable voice. "What has fashion to do with it? Surely we can drink what we like?"

"Oh to hell," said Bill Ferris impatiently. Then, "I'm sorry, Mollie. I'm neglecting you. What will it be?"

Mollie Westerly had changed her manner with her clothes

150

since this afternoon and returned to her crisp almost harsh way of speaking.

"Gin on the rocks," she said appropriately.

"I'll have the same," Stanley announced.

There was silence when everyone had been given a drink.

"I miss the old archery," said Bill, breaking it. "I was getting quite hot in the last few weeks."

"Darling, anyone would think you were a marksman, the way you talk," said Stella sharply. "You were only just above average. Kneller was a far better shot."

"Perhaps. Shooting at targets. Give me *tir à la perche*. I could have seen him off at that."

"Really, darling, you *do* bore me when you talk like that. Who wants to hear how brilliant you were at shooting birds out of trees? All Mr. Deene wants to know is whether you shot Sime."

"And if so, *why*?" added Carolus disconcertingly.

There was an uncomfortable pause.

"I've got the beset alibi in the world for that," said Bill Ferris. "I *couldn't* have done it. Not because of circumstances, or times, or anything like that, but because I just haven't the skill."

"My husband has a theory about Sime's death," said Stella.

"It's an anti-theory. I just don't believe that Sime was shot from the archery lawn."

"No?" said Carolus watching him intently.

"No. I think someone went up to his window, pulled the curtains aside and shot him from there. Point blank range. That would account for the accuracy and force of it."

"You don't think such a person would have been seen?"

"Not necessarily. If it was early in the afternoon, before any of us were out on the archery lawn."

"What about Matron?"

"Matron is only human. . ."

"Human?" said Mollie.

"Biologically, I mean. Even Matron's eyes, trained and skilled and indefatigable as they are, cannot see round corners. Sime's window was invisible from hers."

"But not the approach to it," said Stanley. "If someone did what you suggest he would have had to carry a bow and arrow from the summer-house."

"And back," said Carolus.

"Difficult, but not impossible," Bill Ferris pronounced. "Much easier to believe than that someone shot him as accurately as that from the archery lawn."

Carolus seemed determined to be difficult.

"If he went to the summer-house as you say before anyone was out, he couldn't have got a bow and arrows. Because Kneller kept it locked."

Kneller's name produced a thoughtful silence and after a few moments Carolus returned to the attack.

"What about the curtains?" asked Carolus. "Jumbo Parker drew them over before two o'clock to allow Sime to sleep. They were still pulled close at three when two boys came down from the cricket field to speak to him."

"Why not? My man could have pulled them again from the outside, couldn't he?"

"But they had been pulled *back* when Duckmore found Sime dead at four fifteen," Carolus pointed out.

"I thought it was Mayring who found him dead."

"Duckmore had found him already. How did the curtains get pulled back according to your theory?" Carolus asked Ferris. "If your murderer had done his job before you were all on the archery lawn at three, or thereabouts, and Chavanne found the curtains closed at three, who pulled them back before four?"

152

"Perhaps they weren't back. Duckmore's not very reliable, poor chap. He could have pulled them back himself."

"He could, but he didn't," said Carolus curtly.

"What's your theory, then, Deene?" asked Bill Ferris. He spoke with good humour but also with a note of challenge.

"Don't be silly, darling," said Stella. "You don't expect him to come out with it at this stage, do you? They never do. That all comes with the denouement. Mr. Deene's a professional, remember."

"Oh no," said Carolus, "A free-lance amateur."

"But you have the professional approach. You see all, hear all, and say nothing."

"I know enough to look for a motive every time," said Carolus quietly, his eyes never leaving the group.

Bill Ferris laughed noisily.

"Then you must have the hell of a job this time," he said. "There wasn't anybody who hadn't a motive. . ."

"For murder?" asked Carolus.

"Well, perhaps not for killing the bastard. But everyone had something against him."

"Had you?" asked Carolus in the same mild voice.

It was evident that they all thought the question in the worst taste. Glances were exchanged and Bill Ferris looked uncomfortable.

"I couldn't stand the fellow," he said. "Now, what about another drink?"

The moment was lost, passed over but not altogether forgotten. There was a certain restraint over them as a second round was poured.

Stanley tried to relieve this by asking Bill Ferris if he thought the school, as a flourishing preparatory school, could survive the scandal.

"Difficult to say," said Ferris. "We haven't taken Patrick away yet, as you know, but then we're here to keep an eye on him. He's more interested in playing Quince the Carpenter than anything else at the moment."

"Good idea, that, of Mayring's," said Stanley. "The little wretches have almost forgotten about Sime already."

"Whether other parents will feel like that I can't say. I think it depends very much on the findings at the Inquest on Thursday. Nobody will feel very easy at having a son at a school where there has been a murder."

"Personally, if I knew nothing of it at all, I should be more worried by a fatal archery accident where my son was," said Stella.

"You may be right," said her husband. "But we know it couldn't have been an accident, don't we Deene?"

"It couldn't have been a stray arrow," agreed Carolus.

Bill Ferris stuck to his point. "I'm convinced that if they find on Thursday that Sime was murdered it will empty the school."

"It's a pity, in a way," said Stella. "I don't want Patrick's education interrupted. And there's no doubt that St. Asprey's had a high standard of teaching."

"Teaching—yes. Sconer himself, that is. They've had more scholarships than most schools. Sime wasn't anything like as good as he was cracked up to be," said Bill Ferris. "Or as good as Sconer thought him."

"Do you think he really did? I often wonder," said Stanley. "He certainly listened to Sime as though he was mesmerized by the fellow. But Mrs. Sconer had his measure. She wasn't fooled by him."

"You're prejudiced, Jim," said Mollie Westerly.

"Perhaps. But I knew his work. If you really want to know what I think, it is that Mrs. Sconer wanted badly to get rid of Sime and Sconer for some reason didn't, and built

154

up this idea of him being irreplaceable as a teacher as an answer to her."

"I suppose you got that from Matron?" said Mollie unkindly.

"Did Matron know you were coming here this evening?" asked Bill Ferris.

"She didn't but there isn't the smallest doubt that she knows by now we're here," said Mollie.

"How?"

"How does Matron know? You might as well ask 'what song the Syrens sang, or what name Achilles assumed when he hid himself among women'," replied Mollie with unexpected aptness. "She knows about it all, she knows, she knows," she misquoted confidently and no one disputed it.

Chapter Fourteen

Carolus, coming somewhat late to breakfast next morning, noticed an air of tension among the boys and an empty chair where Matron usually sat.

"Please, sir, Chavanne's going to get the stick after breakfast," Lipscomb informed him.

"Most suitable," said Carolus stirring his unduly weak tea.

"He pulled Matron's chair away," Lipscomb went on, "just as she went to sit down. She went a most terrific crasher."

"I don't think that was very funny," said Carolus.

"Please sir, nor did she, sir. She went most terrifically red in the face. She told Mrs. Sconer and Mrs. Sconer told Mr. Sconer to give Chavanne six of the best."

"Is this true, Chavanne?"

"It's frightfully unfair, sir. I was only rehearsing 'Then slip I from her bum, down topples she'."

"Don't be vulgar, Chavanne."

"Please sir, that's not vulgar. It's Shakespeare."

156

"Thank God the two are sometimes synonymous," said Carolus. "Now finish your breakfast."

"I bet Mr. Sconer lays it on terrifically hard," said Lipscomb enthusiastically.

"Bet he doesn't. Bet he's only doing it because Mrs. Sconer told him to," retorted Chavanne less confidently.

"Bet he gives you six terrifically juicy ones."

Carolus did not wait to hear the sequel but went straight to his car. He had warned his temporary colleagues that he would be away that day, and he knew the route he must take. Through the brilliantly sunny air of that perfect June morning he drove happily, making for the village of Bucksfield in Somersetshire.

Was it natural, Carolus wondered, for one on such a morbid errand to feel insuppressible *joie-de-vivre*? But this was the first really warm day of summer, and the Cotswolds smiled under a blazing sun. Moreover, Carolus was deeply interested in the case he was investigating which had all the teasing perplexities he loved and, as yet at least, no very tragic features. Besides, he had almost reached the point of tying up loose ends.

He found Bucksfield to be a small sleepy village dominated by a huge grey house built in the 1870's. This was Holly House, one of the most famous private mental homes in England.

Carolus knew the professional secretiveness of such places, how the identities of the inmates were concealed, how visitors were treated with suspicion. He sat in his car looking at the grey pile surrounded by lawns and rhododendrons with an almost defiant absence of wall or railing. It was all very expensive-looking and not too gloomy in the sunlight but it was impossible not to have doubts and unhappy imaginings about the interior.

Carolus made no attempt to enter but following the prin-

157

ciples he had learned from previous cases he drove to the local inn, the Fox and Geese. He found a somnolent landlord of immense girth who spoke huskily and without much animation. Carolus ordered his drink and the two stood alone in the room eyeing one another at intervals. Was it necessary to start with the weather? Carolus wondered, then decided against it. The landlord did not look as though he had energy to spare for more than essentials.

"Do they allow visitors at Holly House?" he asked.

The landlord raised a sleepy eyelid and said, "Not if they can help it."

"Do you get any customers from up there?"

"Cases, you mean? No. Can't say we do. Not cases. One or two of the staff look by."

"I want to talk to someone who works there," confided Carolus.

"Who?"

"Doesn't really matter as long as it's someone who has been there some years."

The landlord nodded and fell into a not unpromising silence. He was evidently thinking.

"Tell you what," he said presently. "There's Tom Hopper."

"Who's he?"

"One of the nurses. Red-headed chap. Walks with a little bit of a limp. Always whistling. Lives next door to the post office."

"Yes?" said Carolus.

"Wears an old-fashioned watch-chain. Talks very loud. Rolls his own cigarettes. Likes a pint or two."

"What about him?" asked Carolus.

"He comes in every morning. Regular as clockwork. He worked at Holly House for a long time. He may be able to tell you what you want to know."

"Thanks."

"Likes a pint or two," said the landlord who once launched on identification did not seem anxious to abandon it even at the cost of repetition. "Rolls his own cigarettes. Talks very loud. Wears one of those old-fashioned watch-chains. Lives next door to the post office."

"Always whistling?" queried Carolus.

"That's it. You've got him. Walks with a bit of a limp. Red-headed chap. Tom Hopper his name is."

"You think he'll be in this morning?"

"Sure to be. Comes in every day. You can't mistake him."

"No. I'm sure I can't."

"You'll see him coming down the road in a minute. Walks with a bit of a limp. . ."

"Will you have a drink?" suggested Carolus hurriedly.

"Thanks. I'll have a drop of bitter. Yes, you'll know him as soon as you see him. Tom Hopper, his name is. Wears an old-fashioned. . ."

"Lovely morning, isn't it?" asked Carolus fervently.

"This looks like him coming up the road now. Yes, that's him. You talk to him about Holly House. He'll tell you. Some of the things he says about the Cases would make you die laughing."

"I don't somehow think so," said Carolus.

Tom Hopper when he entered answered to the landlord's description in every detail, but he also had very foxy little eyes.

"Gentleman was asking about Holly House," said the landlord. "I told him he should ask you."

"Ah," said Tom Hopper.

"You know more about it than anyone," went on the landlord.

"Was it about one of the Cases?" Tom Hopper asked Carolus.

"Yes, I suppose it was," Carolus admitted.

"Not supposed to talk about any of the Cases," said Hopper.

"Have a drink?"

"I don't mind. Only we have to be careful about discussing the Cases. Are you from a newspaper?"

"No. I have personal reasons for asking. Do you remember a man named Duckmore?"

Hopper set down his glass and blinked at Carolus.

"That's a funny thing," he said.

"What's that, Tom?" asked the landlord.

"There was another chap asking about him a couple of months back. Big chap. Wanted to know all about him."

"Were you able to tell him."

"Oh yes. Of course I was. I knew Duckmore well. He was one of my special charges. But we're not supposed to talk about the Cases."

"You'll lose nothing by doing so to me," said Carolus significantly.

"Thank you," said Hopper. "What was it you wanted to know?"

"He was a voluntary inmate?"

"They all are, at Holly House. Or so they say. It's mostly their families put them there. He came on his own and stayed two or three years. Very unusual case."

"Why?"

"You know he'd been in the nick, don't you?"

"I suspected it."

"It wasn't very much. Failure to pay maintenance. Contempt of Court. Something like that. He'd had a very difficult married life, I gathered, and it had gone to his brain. He'd got what we call obsessions."

"What kind of obsessions?"

"So far as I could make it out this man Duckmore was

160

well off. Went to the university and got his degree and that. Then he married this woman."

"Which woman?"

"This woman he was married to. She gave him hell, I understand. Years of it. Nag, nag, nag. You know what that means?"

"I've no experience but I can guess."

"On at him all the time. Never a moment's peace. Till he up and left her and the child and all. There was a big case about it and he was ordered to pay her so much a week."

"That was surely the right thing?"

"He didn't think so. Mind you, I only know all this from what I was told. He said he'd rather go to prison than pay her anything. In the end they put him in Brixton Gaol. That quite turned his head for a time and he got these obsessions."

"But what were the obsessions?" asked Carolus patiently.

"He thought he'd murdered her. Never done anything of the sort but he got it in his head he had. What we call a Guilt Complex."

"Oh, you do?"

"Yes. That's what we call it. I've known others like that only his was the worst case I've ever known. Went on about it, time and again. How he'd gone after her with a hatchet. All the time she was as much alive as you or I. She used to come down and see him to show him he was making it up. He'd talk to her for half an hour, then next day he'd start all over again. How he'd hacked her to pieces and that. You couldn't do anything with him."

"No?"

"There was one doctor took a special interest in him and after about a year he began to get better. His wife had divorced him by now and married again. After a lot of treatment you could tell he was going to be all right. Wonderful what they can do nowadays."

"I'm sure."

"Then he got it into his head he wanted to be a parson. Quite sensible about it, he was. Not religious mania or anything, though we *do* have plenty of that sort. Just quietly began studying for it. Before he left here he was as sane as you or I. Mind you, he was always a nervous sort of chap. But now he was on the ball. The doctor told me he'd be all right and he thanked me for all the care I'd taken of him. Well, I had at the beginning. When he had those obsessions. You get all sorts in my job."

"Did he confide in you?"

"I suppose you'd call it that. He said the one thing he wanted in life was to be a parson and help others. Then he went to see these people. . ."

"What people?"

"Church people. A Bishop, I think it was. They told him he had better take some other job for a time, like a schoolmaster, to make sure he was all right. Couldn't have anything go wrong once he was a parson, could they?"

"I suppose not."

"He told me all this not long before he left here, and said that was what he was going to do, get some job in a private school where they wouldn't ask too many questions. He seemed quite hopeful and cheered-up about it."

"Did you ever hear from him afterwards?"

"Not for a long time I didn't."

"But eventually?"

"That's the funny part. Only about a week ago I got a letter." Hopper broke off. "We're not supposed to talk about all this you know. I don't know whether I ought to tell you any more."

"I've told you, you will lose nothing."

162

"I daresay. But I'd like to know how much I'm not going to lose," said Hopper quietly while the landlord served someone in the public bar.

"A fiver," suggested Carolus, and Hopper nodded.

"Well, this letter came only a few days ago. It was a surprise to me, I can tell you. What do you think he said?"

"That he expected to be coming back to Holly House?"

"That's just what he did say. It gave me quite a shock. I thought when he left here he'd be all right. But there you are."

"Did he give any reason?"

"Only that he'd had a lot of worry lately. Wanted a rest, he said. Could he have his old room back? I showed it to the doctor who'd treated him before and he was quite upset about it. He thought he must have been under some terrible strain. Anxiety neurosis, *we* call it. You get the idea?"

"Broadly, yes," said Carolus. "And that is all you have heard of Duckmore?"

"Yes. I'm not much of a one for writing letters myself, so I didn't answer his. It wasn't for me to tell him anything about having his room back. He'd have to write to the Lady Almoner for that."

"During all the time he was here, did Duckmore ever show any tendency towards violence?"

Hopper considered this.

"Well, not in the sense that he *did* anything violent, no. Not like some of them. You have to have your wits about you with one or two, I can tell you. Manic depressives is the name we give to them. Only the other day. . ."

"But Duckmore showed no symptoms of this?"

"No. I'm not saying he did. But he thought and talked about violence—homicide particularly. He took a big interest in murder cases in the newspaper."

"I like a good murder, myself," said the landlord who

163

had returned. "Like to read about it, I mean. What about this man in France who did for seven—all in the same village? Interesting, anything like that."

"That was the sort of case Duckmore went for. Anything out of the way. He once tried to work out how many different ways there was to put an end to anyone and covered I don't know how many sheets of paper with lists. We had to stop him doing this. But he went on talking to me about it. Everything from strangulation to poisoned arrows."

"*Poisoned* arrows?"

"You know—like some of these wild people use up the Amazon," said Mr. Hopper rather vaguely. "But he was all right when he went from here. That I can answer for."

Carolus prepared to leave the pub having passed Hopper his Judas-money.

"There's a lot more I could tell you," said Hopper as he pocketed this.

"About Duckmore?"

"Not just about Duckmore. Some of the others are worth talking about, I can tell you. We had one man. . ."

"I must run along, I'm afraid," said Carolus nodding hurriedly to the landlord. "I'm sure you have a fascinating life but unfortunately at the moment I haven't time to hear about it."

"I was going to tell you about this fellow. Every evening about the same time. . ."

"*Good* morning," said Carolus, and managed to get out of the bar-room.

He drove back with less exuberant thoughts than those he had enjoyed on setting out. He had found Mr. Hopper depressing and sordid and his information, though it was valuable, seemed cheerless.

He stopped for a poor lunch at a wayside hotel and afterwards sat alone in a room called the Residents' Lounge drinking coffee and thinking. Execept for a few stray ends the case was now clear but he did not like the turn it had taken. He wondered whether Detective Superintendent Osborne saw the evidence in the same light. It would be a relief if the policeman made the arrest he expected and enabled him, Carolus, to return to Newminster as soon as the Inquest was over. But he did not believe Osborne yet had all the necessary information.

Back at the school that afternoon he found the grounds deserted except for Horlick the gardener, a youngish and rather handsome man.

"The boys are all up at the cricket field, I suppose?" he said, by way of passing conversation, to Horlick.

"S'right," said Horlick, continuing his work.

"Your roses are *some*thing," he continued.

Horlick did not deny this—or admit it, either.

"Much troubled with pests?"

"Not insects," retorted Horlick.

"Boys?"

"Not extra."

"Your wife works at the school too, I believe?"

"Aye."

"I should like to have a chat to her, sometime."

"She's not the chatty sort," said Horlick.

"No? I'm trying to find out who killed Sime."

Horlick grew suddenly loquacious, at least for him.

"She doesn't know anything," he said. "She never saw or heard anything. She wasn't here that afternoon. She wouldn't tell you if she did."

"Sensible woman. I suppose she has told the police anything she knows."

"She doesn't know. Not a thing. I told you."

"And you, Horlick?"

"Me? What should I know about it?"

165

"I understand you have been known to try your hand at archery."

"May have done. Once or twice."

"Did you happen to go up to the archery lawn on the afternoon Sime was killed?"

"I was there for a minute. I told the police."

"What did you go there for?"

"I'd found one of their arrows."

"Where?"

"Nowhere you'd expect to find it shooting from where they did."

"You mean somewhere on this side of the house?"

"Just about a yard from where you're standing."

"When did you find it?"

"On Saturday morning, if you want to know."

"The morning after the murder?"

"S'right," said Horlick and picking up his tools walked away.

Chapter Fifteen

"I want to tell you everything. Everything," said Duckmore.

He was sitting in an upright chair in Parker's room late that Tuesday evening. He had knocked on the door ten minutes earlier and asked permission to come in and 'ask you Men for advice'. Parker had given him a drink which at first he refused and now, a little flushed and with spasmodic movements of the hands as he talked, he explained that he had a confession to make.

Carolus did not show himself in the least sympathetic.

"You have a habit of making confessions, Duckmore," he said coldly. "You used to confess to killing your wife."

Duckmore showed no surprise that Carolus knew this, and no indignation.

"I know. But that was quite different. It was an obsession I had. While I was in a mental home. I was in an abnormal condition at the time. Now I know precisely what I have to say. I have no illusions at all."

Carolus looked at him and slowly nodded.

"Very well," he said, less sharply. "Let's hear what you want to tell us."

"I can trust you both," said Duckmore, looking first into Parker's good-natured face, then less confidently to Carolus. "It's rather a long story. But when you've heard it you'll understand all that has happened here this term. And you'll know who killed Sime, if you don't know already."

There was a suggestion of interrogation in these last five words but Carolus did not rise to it.

"A year ago," began Duckmore, "I was a reasonably happy man. I had got over all my mental troubles and got this job which I intended to keep for a year or two before going into the Church."

"Did Sconer know your history?" asked Carolus.

"He knew only that I had been ill for two years. But to get a man with my degrees to teach in a preparatory school is unusual and he did not enquire too closely. I don't think he has ever had cause to regret it—till now. I did my job conscientiously and was quite successful with the boys. Don't you think so, Jumbo?"

Parker nodded.

"I've always said you were a good teacher."

"I did feel rather under false pretences sometimes. You see, it wasn't only the mental home—I'd been in gaol, too. You didn't know that did you?"

"I suspected it," Carolus said, "when I heard how in moments of strain you would stand counting the boys as they passed through a doorway. I've learned enough about prison to know that screws do that all the time."

"It was only on a maintenance order," said Duckmore. "But anyhow, all that was forgotten. Left behind. I came here, I liked the life, I got on with everyone at first—even Matron. I was determined to do my two years' 'test' period, then take Orders. It was all I wanted from life.

168

"You see, I was in touch with Sturgess Rimmer. You know all about him."

Carolus knew the name as that of a controversial Anglican bishop who delighted the Press by having an opinion on everything and being delighted to express it whenever he was approached for an interview.

"He has taken an interest in me. It was he who suggested that I should teach for a couple of years. Afterwards he will find work for me in his diocese. He had great confidence in me. So you see, all was going well.

"Then, towards the end of last term, Sime heard me mention the village of Bucksfield. It was at tea in the common-room one day and I was talking to Stanley. I said something quite casual about the architecture of one of the houses. But Sime picked it up at once.

" 'Bucksfield', he said. 'That's where there's a big mental home, isn't it?'

" 'I've no idea', I told him. But it was no good. I saw him staring at me and knew I was giving myself away.

"Two days later he tackled me when I was alone. 'You were *in* that mental home, weren't you, Duckmore?' he said. I had to admit I'd been there for a short time as a voluntary patient. He did not say any more at the time. But during the holidays he must have gone over there and found out everything. It wouldn't be very difficult. The male nurses there were a poor lot and would talk to anyone about their work. He heard it all—about the delusions I'd had about my wife, everything. And he came back this term resolved to take advantage of it."

"I thought there was something of that sort going on," said Parker.

"The first thing he did was to ask me for money. I thought he meant a small loan to tide him over till he could ask Sconer for an advance, and I offered to lend him £50.

He laughed at that. Then he told me he meant to own this school before long. Finally he threatened to tell everyone what he'd learned about me.

"I was not so worried about that. After all, Sturgess Rimmer knew it already. So I told him he could tell whom he liked. He said 'You'll be sorry for this, Duckmore'.

"Then things began to happen. You know what I mean, Jumbo? Appearances and noises. The killing of Mayring's dog. The rabbits. The rat in Matron's bed. And after every one of these Sime affected to suspect me. I would protest and he would say—'Well, who else could it be? With your history. You'd never convince anyone it wasn't you. And that would put a stop to your 'test' period, wouldn't it?'

"At last I gave him money—a thousand pounds. I thought, like everyone else who has been blackmailed, that I would get some peace for that. Then, immediately afterwards, there was that face at the dormitory window and he started all over again. There seemed to be nothing I could do."

"Have another drink?" said Parker, and Duckmore nodded distractedly. He was in a state of high nervous tension.

"You see," he went on. "I began to wonder whether I was doing these things. As Sime said, who else would? I never really suspected him. Not because he wasn't bad enough but I couldn't somehow see him wandering about at night doing these senseless things. Once or twice I listened at his door and heard him snoring. I got into a dreadful condition of nerves. At last. . ." Duckmore hesitated and when he spoke again it was almost in a whisper. "At last I decided to kill him."

"When did you make that decision?" asked Carolus.

"I don't quite know. I think I'd had it in my head for a long time. But I couldn't see how to do it. It must have been just before you came here that I finally made up my mind.

"It was the archery that suggested the way to do it. You see when I was at the university I had been very keen on it. At that time I was a really good shot. I won a couple of championships. When Kneller started it here I said nothing about that. I was out of practice and in any case too jumpy to be much good at first. But I knew that if I *had* to make one really accurate shot I could do it. And without telling anyone I practised."

"How do you mean? There was no time when you could go out there alone."

"No. But I practised when the rest were there without letting them know what I was doing. I would take a spot on the edge of the target and shoot at it. When I hit it, it looked like a rotten shot. Then I'd take one on the other side of the target. Then I'd send one off the target altogether. No one dreamed I was getting more and more accurate until I knew I could be sure of myself at any range between forty and eighty yards."

"On the range," Carolus pointed out.

"Well, yes."

"With an ordinary arrow. Not a broadhead."

"That's so."

"Was this before Sime was laid up?" Carolus asked.

"I started before then. I had a vague idea much earlier. But when he was laid up and sat up in bed watching us I knew just how to do it. I meant to shoot him through the heart.

There was a long silence in the room and Carolus did nothing to break it. He was watching Duckmore with undisguised interest.

"I went about it carefully," Duckmore went on at last. "I discovered that when the five of us stood in a row to

171

shoot at our five targets, two of us were invisible from the house. We all knew that Matron observed everything she could and she could see three of the archers. So I waited for the ideal conditions. These were, one, that there should be *no more than five people on the archery lawn,* all archers; two, that Sime's curtains should be drawn back, leaving him exposed to those on the archery lawn though behind us as we shot for the target; and three, that I could fire from one of the two points at which I was invisible from the house. These conditions never came together till the afternoon of Sime's death.

"As you know, we shoot six arrows each at the target and when all five of us have shot we walk down together and recover them. This is exciting—you go forward to count your score. You will find that people who have just shot and are walking towards their targets seldom take their eyes from these.

"For several days I was prepared. That is to say I took one of the concealed points and had seven arrows instead of six. But there was always someone standing about watching. However, that afternoon there were just the five of us. People had been about—even Sconer came out that afternoon—but just before four o'clock, before Mayring came down from the cricket field, conditions were ideal. I fired my six arrows, then pretended to be tying my shoelace while the others walked forward towards the target. I took my seventh arrow. . ."

"A broadhead?" asked Carolus.

"No. No. The arrow we use on the range. I couldn't have been accurate with a broadhead. Its altogether different. I turned round to face the house, and shot. I was aiming at the heart but I have a tendency to shoot high. My arrow pierced Sime's throat. He must have died immediately."

"Suppose you had missed?" said Carolus.

"Suppose I had."

"You would have been seen."

"No. As I explained. . ."

Carolus interrupted harshly.

"Not by Matron. *But by Sime himself.* Didn't you think of that?"

"He was probably asleep," said Duckmore. "He used to sleep in the afternoon."

"But how did you know that? Had you done anything to ensure that he would be asleep?"

Duckmore looked rather baffled.

"No," he said. "I was quite sure of myself. And as you know, I didn't miss." He went on hurriedly. "I didn't wait to see then, of course. I hurried after the others and caught them up about halfway down the range. We were all chattering about our scores."

"Who were the five?" asked Carolus.

"Mollie Westerly, Stanley, Bill and Stella Ferris and myself."

"Where was Kneller?"

"He'd gone to his cottage for a few minutes. He was worried about his wife. When we came back to the shooting line Mayring was there, just down from the cricket field. He wanted to shoot so I told him to take my place, and they started again.

"I walked away quite casually. As I crossed to the house I saw Kneller coming back from his cottage. Then I went into the staff block. I looked into the common-room but no one was there. Then I tapped on Sime's door."

"Why did you do that?"

Again Duckmore looked confused.

"I don't quite know," he said. "Habit perhaps."

"Did you know you had hit him?"

"Oh yes."

173

"You could see from where you shot?"

"Yes, I. . ."

"You were quite sure?"

"Yes, but of course I couldn't be certain that he was dead. Anyway, I tapped and naturally there was no answer. I slowly pushed the door open. Then I was nearly sick. Well, *you* saw him. He was dead and there was a great deal of blood. I did not go near him but quickly closed the door and went to my own room. Then I *was* sick."

Parker nodded sympathetically.

"It was a beastly sight," he said.

"I realized that I must pull myself together," went on Duckmore. "I was supposed to be on duty in the dining-room for the boys' tea. I had a wash and hurried along but the boys had been in for several minutes and Matron was there. She said something about my being late but I didn't take much notice. I was thinking of what I had seen in Sime's room.

"Then suddenly, after the boys came out of the dining-room, something in me seemed to snap altogether and I knew I had to get away. I did not think where or how—just to get out of the school. I took nothing with me—I really didn't know quite what I was doing. I kept seeing Sime. I had no plan. I remember rushing down the drive and out into the road. Then I met you, Deene."

"Yet almost the first words you said to me were that you had *not* killed Sime," said Carolus.

"Were they? I don't remember. I was in a terrible state. I wasn't going to admit it. I expect I said it was an accident. I'd always hoped it would be taken for an accident."

"You did."

"I didn't know what I was saying. But I've told you the truth now."

"Why?" asked Carolus.

"I wanted to get it off my chest. I couldn't go on like this. If you had seen him!"

"Why did you tell us? Instead of the police?"

"Oh, I'm going to tell the police."

"When?"

"Tomorrow."

"Why not tonight? It's not eleven o'clock yet."

"No. No. I want time to think. You see, Sturgess Rimmer is coming tomorrow. I want to tell him first and ask him what I should do."

"What can you do, but tell the truth?"

"I know. I know. But I want to talk it over with him. He's a very understanding man."

"So you propose to go through tomorrow, taking your classes and behaving as usual before confessing to murder?"

"It sounds awful when you put it like that, but I've gone so far. This has been on my mind ever since it happened. One more day. . ."

"It's not for me to say anything about it," said Carolus. "But a confession of murder is surely not something to put off, is it?"

"I *will* go tomorrow," said Duckmore, "as soon as the Bishop has gone."

"I think you should go tonight. Or early tomorrow morning."

Duckmore stared at him.

"Is anyone else suspected?" he asked in a horrified voice.

"By the police? I have no means of knowing."

"How can they be? No one else could have done it."

"You mean, no one else is as good a shot as you?"

"No. Not for a shot like that."

Carolus spoke very slowly and carefully.

"Look, Duckmore," he said. "I want to take you back to that afternoon for a moment."

"Please don't."

"It's rather necessary you know. For other people's sake. You remember turning round to shoot that seventh arrow?"

"Yes. Yes."

"What did you see when you turned? Through Sime's window, I mean. You were some forty yards away."

"Forty-five. I had reckoned it exactly. To get my range. I saw *him*."

"You saw Sime? Distinctly? Try to remember."

"I saw the outline. It was all I needed."

"The outline of what?"

"The bed. Sime."

"Could you see his face?"

"Yes. Well . . . I could see where it was."

"If it had been someone else sitting up in that bed—*would you have known*?"

"But I knew it was him."

"Exactly. You shot at an outline. Could you see where your arrow struck?"

"I knew I had hit him."

"Did you? Then? You knew afterwards, of course, because you went into his room. But at the time?"

"I thought I had."

"That's better."

"But I had. We all know that."

"You go to the police tomorrow, Duckmore. Whatever anyone tells you. *Go to the police*."

A very obstinate look came into Duckmore's face.

"Not till the afternoon," he said, "when I've seen Sturgess Rimmer."

"I can't say any more then. But I warn you, you're

delaying something you ought not to delay, and it may have serious consequences."

Carolus stood up.

"I'm going to bed," he said and nodding to the two men, left them together.

Chapter Sixteen

Though St. Asprey's School had passed through many strange events that term, the next twenty-four hours, the hours before the Inquest, were certainly the most curious period of time in its history, a history, no one could help feelng, which was rapidly coming to a close.

The boys seemed to remain totally unaware that a climax impended and one would have said they had already forgotten Sime. At breakfast they bombarded Carolus with questions and during the morning classes of a sort continued. Mrs. Sconer was absent from breakfast and this seemed to put Matron on her mettle. From her table she could observe most people in the room and like those of the Last Duchess, her looks went everywhere.

It was during the Break that Carolus received a summons. A small breathless boy came to him and said—"Please sir, Mrs. Sconer wants to speak to you."

"Thank you for bringing the message," said Carolus, who was glancing at *The Times* crossword.

"Please sir, she said at once," said the small boy. "She said in the rose garden," he added.

Tribal junketers, 5 letters. Too easy. Kurds. Statue of A.E.W. 5 hyphen 5. What was the matter with the setter today? He was giving it away. Stone Mason, of course.

"Please sir, are you going?" asked the small boy, awed by Carolus's bravado.

From childhood Carolus could hear echoes of the laws of courtesy—never keep a lady waiting.

"Yes," he said smiling to the small messenger. "I'm going now."

He found Mrs. Sconer deftly applying a pair of secateurs to errant growths.

"Good morning, Mr. Deene," she said graciously. "I wanted to see you. The Inquest is tomorrow."

"Yes," said Carolus.

"Everything depends on the verdict."

"You mean, the school," said Carolus rather crossly.

"Everything," repeated Mrs. Sconer in the voice of Lady Macbeth. "What will that Verdict be?"

"Murder, of course," said Carolus. "I've told you all along."

"You are not disposed to modify your opinion?"

"No."

"In spite of your stay among us? I thought that as you became acquainted with our small happy community, you would see how impossible it was that anyone here should wish ill to another. At least," added Mrs. Sconer more realistically if less explicitly, "at least not to *that* extent."

"You take a rather rosy view, don't you? It seems to me that anyone might have murdered Sime from sheer distaste. And almost everyone had other motives."

"You are very bitter. You make me regret that I supported your stay here when my husband felt it could serve no further purpose."

"Oh well. I shan't be here much longer."

"I think I ought to tell you that my husband has appealed to Mr. Gorringer to use his influence. He really thinks that your pessimistic outlook threatens the future of St. Asprey's."

Carolus laughed.

"That will tickle Gorringer. He'll be over here as fast as a borrowed car can bring him."

"Exactly," said Mrs. Sconer. "He arrives this evening. He feels that in view of your insistence on the idea of a murder having taken place he should see you before the Inquest."

"No harm in that. Anything else you wanted to see me about? I ought to get across to my class."

"My husband will understand your absence since you are with me," promised Mrs. Sconer grandly. "And there *is* something else I wish to tell you."

"Good. Nice piece of evidence?"

"A very curious circumstance which I have not mentioned till now because I have only just realized that it may be. . ."

"A clue? Then let's hear it."

"It is something that happened on the afternoon of . . . the fatal accident. Someone entered our bedroom."

"Would that be unusual?"

"Unprecedented. Mrs. Skippett does the room in the morning and after that only I and very occasionally my husband go . . . goes . . . go in."

"I see. How do you know of this intrusion?"

"I went up myself after seeing you in the drawing-room. I found one drawer in my husband's chest-of-drawers not properly shut."

"But surely you can't feel *so* sure of Mrs. Skippett's efficiency that you can assume an intrusion by someone else?"

"It is not only that. I opened the drawer and found it disarranged. My husband has a very orderly mind and keeps everything in perfect order. The drawer was in chaos. What is more, *a pair of gloves was missing.*"

For the first time Carolus seemed a little impressed. "How can you be sure of that?" he asked.

"I had checked the contents that very morning."

"Why?"

"I am sorry to say that I had lost confidence in the honesty of Mrs. Skippett. Matron had informed me. . ."

"Yes, yes. I see. Then why do you not suspect Mrs. Skippett of taking the gloves?"

"Because she had finished on this floor before I made my examination. The gloves were removed during the afternoon while she was doing the hall downstairs. She would never have risked a return to it. She would have had to pass Matron's door."

"I see your point. But someone risked it."

"So it appears. The gloves at all events were removed and the drawer left untidy. My husband tells me that he certainly never came upstairs that afternoon."

"That's very interesting. I take it the staff don't leave their clothes at the school during the holidays?"

"Certainly not. They require them, of course. Nor should I encourage anything of the sort."

"So that during the summer term none of them would be likely to have brought gloves?"

"Most improbable. You think one of the assistant masters actually entered my bedroom that afternoon and appropriated a pair of my husband's gloves?"

"Looks like it, doesn't it?"

There was a fighting glint in Mrs. Sconer's eye.

"I can scarcely believe it!" she said.

"Whoever it was must have had urgent need of a pair of gloves," said Carolus casually.

"You understate it. Not once, since St. Asprey's opened. . ."

"But then you haven't had a murder before, have you? The only surprising thing about it seems that the person was not observed."

"You mean by Matron? But Mr. Deene, even Matron hasn't got eyes in the back of her head."

"No? We all have our little limitations, don't we? I must go back to my class."

Before lunch Carolus had an awkward scene with Duckmore. It was raining and unable to escape into the open air, during the twenty minutes between the end of classes and lunch, Carolus found himself trapped by Duckmore in a corridor. He had the feeling that Duckmore was designedly waiting for him there. Certainly he was pale and wretched-looking and his movements were spasmodic and uncertain. There was something almost pleading in his manner.

"I *am* going," he said.

Carolus, somewhat baffled by the situation of a man who had confessed to murder overnight conducting classes of small boys in the morning, made no reply but nodded in what he hoped was an understanding way.

"The Bishop is coming at four," Duckmore added, a sentence which might have been amusingly enigmatic if Carolus had not known the circumstances.

"I shall go as soon as he leaves. You can *take* me if you like." He spoke as though he had to answer to Carolus for any delay or doubt about his reporting to the police.

"I will," said Carolus. "About five?"

He found the whole conversation somewhat macabre.

"Yes. Yes. After the Bishop has gone. He won't stay more than half an hour. Terribly busy man." He turned to admonish two small boys. "Nichols! Stop ragging Winn! You'll make him blub again." Then to Carolus, "Fiends, aren't they? Yes, I'll go with you. You can hand me over yourself. It will be a relief, really."

At lunchtime everything was done to make it seem an everyday occasion. Matron re-appeared, Duckmore sat surrounded by the Junior boys at his table and was audibly discussing cricket, Mrs. Sconer smiled graciously on the scene. An uninformed visitor could never have guessed that the school had been the scene of a desperate murder and that one of the assistant masters was about to confess to it.

Afterwards Carolus found himself alone in the common-room with Parker. The Oldest Assistant seemed very calm.

"What did you think of our friend last night?" he asked, as he lit his pipe.

"I think he should tell the police what he told us."

"Yes. One can't help feeling sorry for him, though. A man who is being consistently blackmailed is under great provocation."

"To murder? I can't agree. He has other remedies. Sime was not a very clever blackmailer."

"I suppose not. But he seems to have been clever enough for Duckmore."

"Duckmore was not the only person at the school he was blackmailing."

"He wasn't?"

"No. He knew about Sally O'Maverick."

"Sally? What about her?"

Carolus knew that he was about to shatter an illusion.

"She underwent an operation," he said gently.

183

"You mean?"

"Abortion."

"Good God!"

"Someone here arranged it and paid for it. Sime knew that. That was his second line of blackmail."

"What a bastard!" said Parker.

"Sime, you mean? Yes, he was."

"Are you sure about this?"

"Oh yes. I've seen Sally O'Maverick's aunt, Mrs. Ricks."

"And you know who it was?"

"Yes."

"So someone else had a motive for murdering Sime besides Duckmore."

"Quite a number of people."

"I suppose it will all come out at the Inquest tomorrow?"

"Most of it, anyway. One must never under-estimate the police. If I could find Mrs. Ricks, so could they."

"I see what you mean. So the school is finished?"

"Not necessarily, I should have thought, but I'm not really competent to judge. I know how you feel about the school, Parker, but for me, you must know, it is of quite secondary importance. I'm concerned with the fact that a man has been murdered."

"I know," said Parker sadly. "I don't expect anyone else to feel as I do. A little private profit-making concern—but I've given more than twenty years of my life to it. I see your point about murder. But do you see mine?"

"Yes," Carolus said. "I do. I'm a schoolmaster myself. But don't be too pessimistic about the school."

Carolus did not see the Bishop that afternoon but in a breathless confidence from Matron just after tea he heard that he had arrived. Matron was as enthusiastic about delivering her news as about gathering it, and baulked of immediately informing Mrs. Sconer (who was entertaining the Bishop to tea) of the afternoon's events she fell back on Carolus.

"Duckmore has been behaving in a most peculiar way all the afternoon," she said, "until the Bishop's car arrived. Fortunately the boys don't seem to realize what's going on because Mayring had his first rehearsal on the cricket field and little Swinton came to me in tears because he's not going to be Peaseblossom or some such thing. Parker has ben in the study with Mr. Sconer for half an hour—what *they* think they can do without Mrs. Sconer is a mystery to me. Now the Bishop's in the drawing-room and they're using the Parents' Tea Service. What will happen tomorrow I *don't* know."

Carolus stared at Matron in wonder at this confession.

"You don't?"

It was not until well after five that Duckmore came to Carolus in the common-room. He looked very calm and serious.

"I'm ready now," he said. "If you'd be kind enough to drive me down to the village. I'm told that the Detective in charge of the case is staying at the local policeman's cottage. I hope he'll be there now."

"If not I'll run you into Woldham," said Carolus.

As they went to the car Carolus was aware of a face at Matron's window, but even Matron might not yet have realized where they were going. Or had she?

Carolus was relieved to see Osborne's car outside the cottage distinguished by a sign, County Police. He asked for Osborne and the local policeman's wife took them into a small sitting-room where Osborne sat alone over the remains of a high tea. Carolus said nothing, waiting for Duckmore to make his announcement.

"Well?" said the Detective Superintendent.

"I've come to give myself up," said Duckmore.

185

Osborne's reaction to this was curious. He seemed to take no notice of Duckmore and his melodramatic announcement, but turned to Carolus.

"What do you want?" he asked.

"Just to hear that," said Carolus. "Now I must be off."

"Are you responsible for this man coming here?"

"Not at all. It is entirely his own idea. I merely drove him here in my car."

"I need not delay you then," said Osborne and turned to Duckmore.

As Carolus left the room he heard Duckmore say distinctly and firmly—"I killed Colin Sime."

On his way back to the school for what he hoped would be his last night there he decided to call at the Windmill Inn. It was as well he did so for leaning over the bar was Mr. Gorringer, his own headmaster. But Carolus's cheerful greeting was checked by a raised hand.

"I am staying the night here," said Mr. Gorringer, "but that is not what brings me here at this hour of the day. When I found that you were not at the school I knew, unhappily, where I was most likely to find you. The local hostelry has ever an almost magnetic attraction for you during your investigations, I find."

"Heard you were coming," said Carolus.

"Against my will," said Mr. Gorringer gloomily. "But what else could I do? When my old acquaintance Cosmo Sconer told me of the position here, I was left with no alternative."

Carolus asked Mr. Pocket, who was eagerly listening to this, for drinks.

"What position?" Carolus asked Mr. Gorringer.

"You can scarcely pretend to be unaware of it, Deene. Sconer informed me that no sooner had you arrived than there was a very unfortunate accident at the school which cost the life of one of his assistants. This you insisted on describing as murder."

"It was murder," said Carolus. "But go on, headmaster."

"When my friend Sconer then suggested that you could be of no assistance to him, indeed that your presence only exacerbated the situation, you threatened to remain in the village. Now, driven to despair, the reputation of his school hanging by a thread, his life's work in jeopardy, with an Inquest impending, he has appealed to me to use my influence with you. He wants you to leave after the Inquest tomorrow."

"That may well be possible," said Carolus.

Mr. Gorringer ignored this.

"I need not say how deeply I have regretted that I ever agreed to your coming here, Deene. It has been an embarrassment to me. I might have known that where you went a violent death would follow. Moreover, I understand that the police in this case are more than usually exasperated by your ill-timed intervention."

"That's true," put in Mr. Pocket unexpectedly from across the bar. "The local man was telling me. What they say about amateur detectives would raise your hair. Well, you can't wonder, can you? They've got a job of work to do."

"Exactly," said Mr. Gorringer, who seemed determined to behave like the Forsaken Merman. "What is more, your own duty calls you. The Upper Fifth. . ."

"I think it is more than probable that the last loose ends will be tied up tomorrow," said Carolus.

"You speak of the last loose ends," said Mr. Gorringer. "Have you then a suspect for this hypothetical murder?"

"A man has just given himself up to the police as the murderer of Sime."

Not only Mr. Gorringer's protruberant eyes but Pocket's

187

beadier ones were, in an expressive metaphor, popping out.

"A man? What man?" cried Mr. Gorringer.

"One of the assistant masters. Character named Duckmore."

"This is a grave matter," announced Mr. Gorringer. "One assistant master in a school confessing to the murder of another. I scarcely know what to say."

"I wonder it doesn't happen more often, myself," said Carolus cheerfully. "Think of Hollingbourne."

"Deene," said Mr. Gorringer. "This is not a matter for frivolous reflections."

"Nor is Hollingbourne, when you come to think of it."

"Enough," said Mr. Gorringer. "Does my poor friend know of this latest and most untoward development?"

"Not from me," said Carolus. "But his wife has an information service such as the C.I.A. might envy. I'd be surprised if Matron hadn't caught a whiff of events."

"Ah. Indeed. That's how the wind blows is it? I often think, my dear Deene, that we should pause sometimes to record our appreciation of our excellent Miss Pink. But whether or not the Sconers have heard rumours it is for you, I feel, to tell them manfully and frankly what has taken place. In a word *allons*!"

Chapter Seventeen

Then suddenly, alone in his room before dinner Carolus had a sense of danger, of resolute black menace deliberately aimed which drove away all more frivolous aspects of the case. It was as if he realized for the first time that this was no delightful problem to be solved with his usual flippancy, but something threatening, directed perhaps at him, something which would need all his courage and resource to defeat.

The people here were, he told himself, a second-rate, tawdry and malicious set such as one might find in the common-room of any preparatory school, but they had qualities unusually bleak about them, their empty lives and their petty hatreds. Forgetting the method used and the skill necessary, there was not one of them who—psychologically —seemed to Carolus incapable of murdering Sime, and there was not one of them whom he believed incapable of murdering again. In a way he liked and was sorry for old Parker, otherwise he found most of them odious and rather sinister.

Moreover he had a feeling that he was being watched for a good part of that day. This might be due to his knowledge of Matron's indomitable powers of observation, but it seemed to him more than that. Someone had him under observation, someone who had reason for concealment, probably, and who was waiting for the moment when Carolus learned something which had so far been kept from him.

He was stretched out in a low armchair of his room as he thought of these things and, instinctively perhaps, he had taken a place from which he could see anyone entering. This part of the house was surprisingly still and silent and he heard no one approaching his door, but as he watched the handle, an old-fashioned oval thing of brass, it began slowly to turn.

Carolus soundlessly straightened himself in his chair. But he realized that as he was smoking a cheroot and his light was on the intruder would be aware of his presence as soon as the door was ajar.

He was. Very slowly the door was pushed forward a couple of inches then as slowly and as silently closed. It took Carolus a second or two to rise from his deep chair and another few to cross the room, but that was enough for the intruder. When Carolus flung open the door he found the landing empty. Shaken more by the swiftness of the other's movement than by the fact that he had come to his room, Carolus poured himself a drink and stood thoughtfully with it in his hand. He would have sworn it was impossible for anyone to be out of sight in that time.

He was angry, too. It was ridiculous to find himself in danger in this wretched little school among a lot of people who apparently acted from more or less petty malice. It was ridiculous and unnecessary. He took from his table a row of four unused postage stamps which he had purchased in the village for some letters he intended to write. Going out in the passage he stuck these to his door and lintel to make a rough temporary seal. Then he went down to the drawing-room and found Mrs. Sconer.

"I want the key of my bedroom," he said.

"Mr. Deene, I find this an intrusion. We do not, for reasons which you should understand, supply the staff with facilities for locking their rooms."

"I'm not interested in your staff. I want the key of the room I am occupying. At once, please. I have good reason for insisting on this."

"Insisting, Mr. Deene?"

Carolus felt vulgar.

"You heard," he said. "You don't want another murder, or attempted murder, in the school do you?"

"You are evidently unaware of what has taken place One of the Men, Duckmore, has confessed to the murder of Sime, and has been taken into custody. It follows that your fears are unnecessary."

"Nothing of the sort follows, I'm afraid. I must warn you, in fact, that there is very real danger for almost every-one connected with the school. That is not my only reason for insisting on locking my room, however."

Mrs. Sconer stared at Carolus.

"Surely," she said less confidently, "we are not going to receive *further* shocks? Where will this end?"

Carolus seemed to cool down.

"I am sorry if I spoke brusquely," he said. "May I please have the key of my room?"

Without another word Mrs. Sconer crossed the room and opened the drawer of a bureau. It held many keys, care-fully labelled. She searched among these and handed him one marked 'Spare Room'.

"I understand you are leaving tomorrow," she said.

"It is probable. Yes."

"Mr. Gorringer informs us that you will be leaving with him, after the Inquest."

Carolus held up the key. "Thank you for this," he said, and left Mrs. Sconer standing, massive and inscrutable, beside the bureau.

The seal had not been disturbed.

At dinner everyone seemed dour and watchful—a most unpleasant atmosphere. Instead of relieving the strain, as one would have thought, Duckmore's disappearance, answering so many questions, seemed to have increased it. No one made any real attempt at conversation, except Mr. Gorringer who boomed with ghastly cheerfulness about county cricket, Mrs. Sconer's roses, politicians as television stars, television stars as politicians, and finally, after failing to awaken the interest of his audience in any of these, Mayring's production of *A Midsummer Night's Dream*.

"A choice of dubious wisdom, I should have thought," he announced. "I disapprove of boys being fairies."

Mayring hotly defended his production and claimed that it had been successul in diverting the boy's attention from —he caught Mrs. Sconer's eye—'other things'.

"Ah yes. No doubt. Admirable," admitted Mr. Gorringer, "but I still think a more virile play should have been chosen."

After dinner Carolus escaped to his room. He felt that he could not take any more from the people among whom he had now spent a week and in his present mood he found Gorringer's pomposity intolerable. There were times when he enjoyed the old-fashioned clichés and Mr. Pooter phraseology of his headmaster, but tonight was not one of them.

He looked from his window and though it was nine o'clock the day was long in dying and the gardens, the road to the village, even the church tower in the distance were discernible. But the air was almost scentless as in most parts of the Cotswolds where the earth is bald. Carolus did not like the area and again he thought that the people he had met here in the school were quite detestable. They were not, any of them, Gloucestershiremen, but the whole atmosphere seemed rancid and Carolus longed to return to his own small house in Newminster.

Not that the case had not interested him—as a problem it had been, and was, fascinating. But there was something abysmally mean and sordid about it. Perhaps that came from the character of the murdered man who seemed to have inspired no affection at all among his colleagues.

Before turning out his light at something past eleven that evening, Carolus locked the door of his room. Then, pulling back the curtains he stood watching an eerie world lit by the intense moonlight of midsummer.

Someone was crossing the lawn, coming towards the house. He recognized Mollie Westerly and watched her as with some difficulty she broke a spike of bloom—lupin, was it?—from the herbaceous border. "In such a night Stood Dido with a willow in her hand," mused Carolus, while from the direction of the staff bungalow came the sound of a door being carelessly closed to suggest that Stanley had just parted from Mollie and gone to his room. Murder and its sequels, detection, confession, Inquest, did not seem to have much effect on that pedagogic idyll, anyway.

Carolus left his window wide open to the night and got into bed, but he did not sleep. He remained for perhaps an hour gently dozing, half aware of the silent house and the shadowy night. Then all his senses were alert in a moment for footsteps were passing his door. They were light and furtive but not slow.

This time he did not rush hurriedly across to open his

193

door, but rose quietly, pulled on a dressing-gown and crossed to the window, taking up a position from which, hidden by one curtain, he could once again watch. He had not long to wait. Though he heard nothing, no closing door or footsteps, he saw a dark outline, the figure of a man, on the grass verge beside the drive. In that curious silver half-light, enough to distinguish only a patch of darkness moving farther from the house, it seemed that the man was gliding without noise over the grass.

In less than two minutes Carolus had pulled on trousers and jacket and carrying his shoes had gone silently downstairs. He closed the front door noiselessly behind him, pulled on his shoes and set off in the direction taken by the man he had seen. Man? At least someone wearing man's clothes. As though this gave him an idea he turned from cover to look up at Matron's window. No one was visible there.

Had he not judged correctly which way his quarry would go he might have lost him, for his range of sight, now that he was on the ground, was not large. But guided by instinct or logic he took the cross-country path which led to the church and before long saw the black outline in motion ahead.

Pursuit became difficult. At first there was plenty of cover and he could remain unseen while not losing sight of the man he was following. But later there was a piece of open ground which he could not cross unobserved. He waited several minutes, calculating the time that it would take his man to have passed beyond sight of the open stretch, then embarked on it. After that he could only continue on the assumption that the trail would lead to the church.

For the rest of the distance he could not be sure whether or not he himself was under observation. Whoever had left the school so secretively might still be well ahead and continuing on his way, but he might have paused beyond the open ground, seen Carolus and taken cover. It was an ugly thought, in no way mitigated by the fact of Duckmore's confession to the murder of Sime.

At last Carolus approached the church. Its grey stone looked bright and silvery and the crosses and headstones of the churchyard stood starkly white against the black-green yews. As though careless of observation now Carolus hurried forward, passed through the lych-gate and reached the porch.

His only means of illumination here was his lighter which, in the way of lighters when one needs them, required petrol. It gave a sickly little light now, but this would cease after a few more strikings. He stretched up and groped in the niche which Spancock had shown him as the hiding-place for the key, but no key was there. It was reasonable to suppose—but not with complete security—that the man he was following had taken it down and used it and was therefore in the church ahead of him.

As soon as he had entered the church, Carolus was sure of this. The place was in darkness and silence but he knew that someone was there. It was a strange fact, he reflected, that the presence of a human being in a closed place, even one so large as this, is nearly always perceptible, and not necessarily by sound, or smell, or sight. A human presence was in some occult way in the air. But he had no idea where that person might be.

Carolus knew from his tour of the church with Mr. Spancock that the lights were controlled from the vestry and he intended to make for the switches as soon as he could see enough to find his way. Meanwhile, having closed the door quietly behind him he stood motionless, waiting for his eyes to accustom themselves to the darkness, or for the other man to give some sensible indication of his presence. He remained there for several minutes till slowly the arches, pillars and pews took vague shapes.

He could hear nothing and could only suppose that whoever was there was aware of him, and was waiting, as he was, for movement. Perhaps behind a pillar, perhaps in a pew, someone must be breathing silently and watching him.

At last there was a tiny sound from the west end of the church where the door to the tower was. The sound, Carolus was almost sure, was of this door being very slowly and gently pulled to.

Now Carolus moved swiftly. Without waiting to use his lighter he groped his way to that door and stood listening, then he started to open it as gently and silently as the other man had closed it. As he did so he heard steps on the stone stairs above him but he must have made some sound for the footsteps ceased and once again there was silence while each strained his ears to listen for the other.

Carolus was the first to move. In complete darkness but with his hearing tensely alert he began very slowly to climb the narrow winding staircase. For some distance he was safe enough for the footsteps he had heard had been almost on the level of the bell-ringers' floor. But there was no sound of movement above him and he knew he was awaited by someone in a stronger position than he was. He ascended as far as he dared, keeping close against the wall to try to gain its support and crawling on all fours as he neared danger. But as he came towards the top of the stairway there was an audible scuffle and he believed that he would be attacked not on the staircase but from the floor of the loft. He knew that his assailant would have every advantage and that he might well share at least the unpleasant experience of Sime in this place.

But would he? The staircase seemed interminable, twist

after twist and Carolus paused every moment to listen. When he believed that he had only a few stairs more to climb he heard more movements from above and knew that he would have no assailant at the stairtop for whoever had been awaiting him had hurriedly crossed the floor of the bell-ringers' loft and was already on the ladder leading to the roof.

Now Carolus abandoned all caution and catlike was after him. As he reached the ladder and started to climb it the trap-door above him was slammed down. He was dealing with someone determined that he should not follow. In a moment Carolus was pushing up the trapdoor, but before it was open three inches his adversary had stepped on it and forced it down on Carolus. It was now immovable and would remain so while the other man stood there. If he was bent on suicide by throwing himself from the tower, as it now seemed sure that he was, he was as trapped as Carolus, and there was a deadlock. Carolus could not join him on the tower but he could not reach the parapet while he stood on the trapdoor.

Meanwhile, Carolus got his breath back and while keeping a continuous upward pressure on the door to know the moment the other left it, he considered the possibilities. While the other remained where he was, he (the other) could not do what Carolus was determined to prevent. But if he stepped off, would Carolus have time to get through and seize him before he threw himself over the parapet? It would be a close thing.

Five minutes passed of this uncomfortable and dangerous deadlock. Then suddenly, incredibly, dramatically there rose to Carolus on his ladder the sound of organ music from the church below. Someone had entered after them and, presumably having gone to the vestry and switched on the lights, was playing a spirited voluntary. At one o'clock in

197

the morning this seemed macabre enough but as an accompaniment to the life-and-death struggle in the tower, of which the organist must surely be unaware, it was spine-chilling.

Then Carolus forgot everything in action. The trapdoor broke free, he flung it open, pushed himself through and was in time, just in time, to seize the other man as he was about to throw himself from the parapet.

But he had reckoned without the strength of a man in the last wild stages of despair and the death wish. He was attacked with the ferocity of a madman fighting for his death. Carolus was lithe and quick and had never lost his skill in unarmed combat, but it seemed that he was not fighting with a creature of flesh and blood but with some monster from science fiction. At one point he found himself underneath while the other pummelled furiously at his stomach and solar plexus, and only by a twist for which his strength was scarcely sufficient did he manage to squirm away and rise to his feet. And all the time he was conscious that he was fighting not only for his own life but for the other's as well.

They swayed to and fro across the roof, neither having breath to use his voice, even if there were any point in shouting. Then, as they approached the parapet farthest from the trapdoor, Carolus slipped and was for a moment at a dangerous disadvantage. If the other had held any weighted thing he could, and undoubtedly would have killed him but he had only his hands and feet. Particularly feet. Carolus saw the leg drawn back and the mighty kick on its way, and that was his last moment of consciousness.

Chapter Eighteen

Returning to a hazed awareness of the world was painful. His confused mind, trying to resume its processes, threw up from the past the memory of a story he had read in a boys' paper thirty years ago. It was called *With a Madman in a Balloon* and was luridly illustrated by a black-and-white drawing of a bearded man in a black cloak and sombrero with fierce eyes and a curved knife who was hacking at the ropes while another cowered in the basket. His struggle on the top of the tower must have called this up from the sub-conscious.

But he was still on the top of the tower, he realized, and the stars he could see were the familar ones of the universe. Moreover he was not alone. Kneeling beside him and supporting his head was Duckmore. He tried to decide whether he had been unconscious for a few moments or a few hours but could make no guess. It might have been days.

"Are you all right, Deene?"

Duckmore's voice sounded remarkably calm and comforting.

"Shall be in a minute. How did you get here?"

"The police let me go. They would not believe what I told them and I see now that they were right."

Carolus tried to work that out but he was still dizzy and confused.

"I *couldn't* have shot Sime," Duckmore went on. "It must have been a delusion due to my state of mind. They kept me till an hour ago then sent me back in a car."

"But what brings you here—to the church?"

"I asked them to drop me here. I don't suppose you will understand this, Deene, but I felt I had to express my gratitude. I had believed I was a murderer you know. So I came in for a while."

"Was that you playing the organ?" asked Carolus, his memory returning.

"Yes. But I had no idea there was anyone up here. I suppose you know that Sconer is dead?"

Again Carolus felt his mind driven back into chaos.

"What?" he asked feebly.

"Yes. At the foot of the tower. He must have . . . fallen from here. I knew nothing till I finished playing and set out for the school. Then I saw something lying there. It was beastly."

Carolus waited.

"I saw what had happened," went on Duckmore. "I thought I ought to come up here and see if there was anyone. I thought he might have been . . . pushed. And I found you."

Carolus tried to stand up but his head seemed to be exploding.

"I must get up," he said feebly. "This must be reported to the police at once."

"Then you didn't . . . push him, Deene?"

"Of course not, you bloody fool. I tried to prevent him committing suicide. But I must get to Osborne."

"I'm thankful for that. I feared . . . I thought. . ."

"So will the police if I don't get to them first. Listen, Duckmore. Do you think you can help me down?"

"I'll try. But that ladder . . . I'm not good at heights."

"Then will you do what I ask you? Go to the Windmill Inn and knock them up. Go on knocking till someone answers. Tell them as little as possible, but enough to stir them up. A man named Gorringer is staying there and Pocket the landlord has a car. Bring them both here, in the car, as quickly as you can. Don't take no for an answer."

"I'll try," said Duckmore.

"You can tell Gorringer it's a matter of life and death."

"All right."

"Leave the trapdoor open. If I feel better while you've gone I shall try to get down to ground level. I'm tired of this tower."

"Take care. . ."

"Yes. Yes. Now hurry. It really *is* a matter of life and death, Duckmore."

When Duckmore's face had disappeared through the trap, Carolus began slowly to move his limbs as though testing each in turn. He realized how urgent it was for him to get on his feet and see Osborne. Duckmore was wholly unreliable—he might take it into his head to go himself to Osborne and talk hysterically of Sconer having been pushed from the tower, and it was by no means inconceivable that Carolus himself would be charged with murder. He had seen in previous cases how the police accepted a theory then built a case to support it.

It took him five agonizing minutes to rise to his feet. His head was still swimming and he felt he could not depend on himself not to faint, perhaps fatally, on the ladder or stairway, but he decided to take the chance. Very cautiously, keeping a firm grip of the sides of the ladder as he did so, he started to step downwards, rung after rung, until he reached the bell-ringer's loft and there leaned against the wall in exhaustion. The worst was yet to come for the spiral staircase had no handrail.

So on all fours and backwards, with no dignity at all and much pain, Carolus made his way down in darkness, then sank into a pew at the back of the nave. The church was brightly illuminated—Duckmore must have switched on every light while he played his *gaudeamus* and forgotten to turn them off when he finished playing.

It seemed a full hour before the church door opened and Mr. Gorringer strode in, followed by Pocket.

Sick and stupid though he felt, Carolus could guess the headmaster's first words.

"Deene, my dear fellow, what is toward?"

"Where is Duckmore?" asked Carolus weakly but with some anxiety.

"Duckmore, who claims to have been released by the police, came to the Windmill Inn and roused us. He explained that you had suffered a serious accident at the top of the church tower, a story which I found improbable, and now see was untrue. . ."

"Quite true. I've just made the descent. But it wasn't an accident. Do you think you can get me to the Windmill?"

Pocket, who looked enthralled by the whole situation, said—"Certainly we can."

"But where is Duckmore?" asked Carolus again in a worried voice.

"Duckmore has gone back to the school. To sleep, he said. Now try to stand up, Deene."

"I can stand up," said Carolus and did so. "But I don't think I can walk far."

"Come now!" said Mr. Gorringer. "Don't forget that at the Windmill refreshment awaits you. Ups-a-daisy! Quick march! Take his arm, Mr. Pocket and we will put him in the car."

Realizing that Gorringer was yet unaware of the broken body of Sconer at the foot of the tower, Carolus tried to occupy his full attention on their way to the lych-gate and succeeded in doing so. With a good deal of unnecessary fuss he was bundled into the back seat of Pocket's car and driven back to the inn. There, in a comfortable armchair in the saloon bar he leant back and drank a little brandy. Revived he turned to Gorringer and Pocket who seemed now no less than wonderstruck.

"Sconer is dead," he told them calmly.

Gorringer goggled.

"Are you serious?" he asked.

"I should scarcely crack jokes about it. He threw himself from the church tower tonight after nearly murdering me."

"Good heavens!" said Mr. Gorringer. "Another death. This is tragic news, Deene. Has his wife yet been informed?"

"Not unless Matron has a telescope which functions at night."

Mr. Goringer seemed to be realizing things.

"You mean to say that the poor fellow's body is still lying out there . . . in the churchyard?"

"It couldn't be anywhere more appropriate, surely. Yes, it is there. No one has touched it, and no one must touch it until the police have examined it. That is what 1 wanted to ask you, headmaster. Would you leave me here and find Osborne, as quickly as you possibly can? It is essential that I give him a statement."

"And who is Osborne?"

"The Detective Superintendent investigating Sime's death. He must hear of Sconer's death from me—otherwise he is quite likely to charge me with murder."

"Do not let us enter realms of fantasy, Deene. You have suffered a shock tonight, but to suggest that my senior history master might be under suspicion. . ."

"Not suspicion. Charged, I said. So please find Osborne at once, headmaster. He may be at the local policeman's cottage or he may be spending the night at Woldham. It's essential that you find him. Take him to the churchyard and show him what's left of Sconer and tell him I want to make a statement about it. He'll have to come here, then."

"I will do as you ask Deene. That is if Mr. Pocket will kindly drive me?"

Pocket nodded.

"I can scarcely absorb the gruesome details. Duckmore released. Sconer a suicide. You the victim of an accident and threatened, you tell me, with a charge of murder. . . These are deep waters, Deene."

Mr. Gorringer shook his head in a sad and puzzled way before he went out followed by Pocket. Carolus heard the car being started and driven away, then let his head fall back and slept.

But he was not left undisturbed. A light in the saloon bar at two o'clock in the morning must have been an unusual sight in Pydown-Abdale and it attracted certain moths. Mrs. Skippett saw it from her cottage a few yards away and decided to hurry round. She woke Carolus by entering.

"Well!" she said. "Whatever are you doing here at this time of night and where's Mr. Pocket? I saw the light on from my cottage and it gave me the flutters. I said to my husband, whatever's that? I said, blazing away at the Windmill like it was illuminated. Something's up, I said and popped on my things to nip across and see whatever had happened. I mean it's enough to give anyone the staggers, isn't it, lights burning and that? Now whoever's this coming in? Oh, it's Mr. Spancock. Good-evening, well, it's morning really, now, isn't it?"

"Extraordinary thing," telegraphed the Rector. "Lights in the church! *All* switched on. Not a soul there. Saw the lights here and came across. What's happened?"

"A good deal," said Carolus wearily. "Pocket has gone for the police. I'm afraid I don't feel up to giving the details till Osborne comes. Why don't you sit down and wait?"

"Think I ought to? Very well. On the spot. In the swim," said Mr. Spancock enigmatically.

"*I* don't know," remarked Mrs. Skippett, as though to keep the ball of conversation rolling. "You can't really tell *what's* going on, can you? Lights and that. I said to my husband, I can't sleep, I said. I shall have to go across and see for myself whatever's the matter, I told him. After all that's happened lately with Sime being murdered and that. It's enough to give you the glooms."

Carolus closed his eyes again and this time must have slept soundly for a short time for he woke to find Gorringer and Pocket in the room.

"All may yet be well," said Gorringer optimistically. "I have interceded personally with the Detective Superintendent. . ."

"Oh God," said Carolus. "Where is he?"

"He has taken charge of proceedings in the churchyard. When I had made my report it set in motion a good deal of telephoning and I understand that the appropriate officials, doctors and experts, photographers and so on are at work on the . . . cadaver. I did not enter the churchyard myself out of respect for my old friend. Rather, I came here to tell you that the Detective Superintendent will be here in due course to take your statement. We must hope that he is satisfied with it."

"Cadaver?" questioned Mr. Spancock anxiously.

"Yes, Sconer's dead," said Carolus scarcely more expansively.

"Well, I never," exclaimed Mrs. Skippett. "Dead, is he? You'd never have thought it, would you? He didn't look to me like one to go off suddenly. Whatever will his wife say about it? But you never know, do you? It might happen to anyone. You're all right one minute and the next you're on your way to the churchyard. That's what I told my husband. It's here today and gone tomorrow, I said and he couldn't only agree with me. I suppose that'll put a stop to the school, then? It's not to be wondered at really, with all that's been going on."

Mr. Spancock seemed to be preparing another question, paring away all verbal fal-lals he asked—"Manner of death?"

"Suicide," retorted Carolus who seemed infected by the Rector's terseness.

"There!" said Mrs. Skippett comfortably. "What did I say? Did for himself, did he? I'm not surprised, really, when you come to think of it. *Her*, I mean, and that Matron. You can't wonder, can you? I mean they never gave him a minute's peace. Oh well, we've all got to go sometime. If it's not one way, it's another. I suppose he thought he might as well get it over once and for all. You never know what people think to themselves, do you? I told my husband. . ."

She was interrupted by the entrance of Osborne and another plain clothes man.

Oborne looked pale but hostile. The small mouth in his large face was tight shut and he moved in a decisive way that suggested authority.

206

"I understand you want to make a statement," he said to Carolus.

"Yes."

"You had better come down to the Station, then."

"Can't do that, I'm afraid. At least not just yet. I've had a bang on the back of the head tonight which knocked me out completely. Besides, I want witnesses present when I make a statement."

"Oh, you do?" Osborne seemed to consider this, then said angrily—"You can have all the witnesses you want. But I warn you, Deene. . ."

"Good. These four will do," and Carolus indicated Gorringer, Pocket, Spancock and Mrs. Skippett.

"I think I ought to tell you that we do not by any means rule out the possibility that Sconer was murdered."

"Of course you don't," said Carolus. "Nor do I."

"He fell from the church tower. There is no evidence that he was pushed over—on the other hand there is no evidence against it. You were with him at the time, I understand."

"In body, yes. But not in mind. I was unconscious."

Osborne was about to answer when a policeman in uniform entered and handed him a paper. He read this and whatever it contained seemed to soften his manner somewhat.

"I see," he said. "You had better make your statement. Please be as brief as possible."

"I will," said Carolus, "but it won't be as brief as either of us would like. The only way I can tell you what happened tonight is to tell you everything, from the beginning, as I understand it."

"I don't want to listen to a lot of circumstantial evidence and theorising," said Osborne sourly.

"And that's just what most of it will be," smiled Carolus.

"Amateur theatricals, I think you called it. But here and there, Superintendent, I hope you may find odds and ends of information you have not got."

Mr. Gorringer unwisely interrupted.

"My friend Deene. . ." he began.

"For God's sake," shouted Osborne brutally. Then, turning to Carolus he said in an exasperated voice—"If you want to make a statement, make one. It's three o'clock in the morning and I've got to be at the Inquest at ten."

Carolus sipped his brandy and began coolly.

Chapter Nineteen

"Sime, 'the most popular master at St. Asprey's' might never have emerged from the common run of teachers in small private schools if the adulation of his pupils had not gone to his head. He was jealous of Sconer and became determined to achieve a partnership and eventually to own the whole school. He publicly boasted that he would do so and get rid of his enemies, thus providing the whole staff with a motive for more than ordinary fear and hatred. Several of them, like Kneller and Duckmore, had reasons for wishing to stay at St. Asprey's quite apart from the posts they held and salaries they earned.

"Once the idea had formed in Sime's mind he looked for ways of fulfilling it. He had no private means but had remarkable determination, a rather sinister kind of success with women and no scruples at all. Given an opening for blackmail he followed it with all the resources of a mean and greedy nature.

"He was blackmailing on three fronts. The first and perhaps the most cowardly blackmail was that of Duckmore. He knew that Duckmore was a fairly rich man and from an unfortunate remark of his about the village of Bucksfield he was able to unearth the whole story of Duckmore's voluntary confinement there in a mental home, his previous history of imprisonment, his delusions about having killed his wife. He also knew that Duckmore's teaching was a 'trial' period before taking Orders—the greatest ambition of his life. He got most of this from an attendant in the mental home named Hopper whom I found easy and cheap to bribe into giving the same information. Hopper remembered his call."

Carolus noted that Osborne made some surreptitious notes here.

"When he found that this information was not enough to make Duckmore disburse large sums, he decided to do a 'gaslight' on him, producing in the school a number of incidents which seemingly could only be the work of a madman and convincing Duckmore that either he had actually been responsible for these or would be suspected or accused of them. He went to great trouble and some expense over these—placing a ladder under one of the windows of a dormitory and appearing at it in horror make-up, perhaps even hiring a costume to appear as a ghostly friar. Sadistic himself he had no difficulty in slaughtering the Angora rabbits and Mayring's dog and so reducing Duckmore to such a condition of nerves that Pocket here described him as 'face white as chalk and hands jumping like a jack-in-the-box, ordering a double brandy'. By this means he succeeded in taking a thousand pounds from Duckmore and anticipated more.

"But this was small game compared with his blackmailing of Sconer. How he came to know the details of Sconer's rather sordid affair with Sally O'Maverick I do not know for I have not yet found the elusive Sally as the police doubtless have."

It would have been scarcely an exaggeration to describe Osborne's face as a mask.

"He must have known that when she left here at the end of last term she was in the family way, for it was generally talked about, as Pocket told me on my first day here. He may even have arranged for the services of the abortionist, described as a negro from Birmingham, probably an African or West Indian medical student needing money. He certainly knew of this gentleman and knew who paid for his services.

"It was obvious to me from the first that Sconer was being blackmailed by Sime. He was suffering from strain far more than the 'nocturnal incidents' would warrant. Mrs. Sconer described him as 'under the spell of Sime' and I discovered, as soon as I took over Sime's classes, that Sconer's defence of Sime, that he was a brilliant teacher whose services he could not afford to lose, was nonsense. He was a bad teacher given to favouritism and personal showing-off which gave him a harmful influence, and his scheduled work was in chaos. Sconer, himself a sound headmaster, *must* have known this, but kept up a pitiful bluff, with his wife and everyone else, simply because Sime was blackmailing him.

"I might not have discovered the details of this unpleasant situation if Sime, crippled by the attempt on his life in the tower, had not been forced to give me a letter to post. I had just arrived and he had no reason to think that I was anything but an ordinary stand-in for him. His letter was to Sally O'Maverick's aunt, on whom, as we shall see in a moment, he was also trying to put the bite. It *had* to go but he dare not give it to any of the staff, for any one of them might have shown it to others. 'Sitck it in your pocket', he said to me. He was taking a necessary chance, and it gave me the address of Mrs. Ricks in Cheltenham."

Though Osborne's face remained expressionless, Carolus guessed that by now Mrs. Ricks was not unknown to him.

"From her next-door neighbour, a woman of almost Matron-like zest for observation, I learned a little more of this—that 'a schoolmaster from the school where Sally had taught' had called, also the 'negro gentleman from Birmingham'. From Mrs. Ricks herself, a righteous woman with secret dipsomaniac tendencies, I learned that Sime had attempted to blackmail her for conniving at the operation for abortion, and that 'someone from the school' had paid for this last. There could no longer be any doubt about the basic situation, Sime blackmailing Sconer, for this alone accounted for all the facts I have set out.

"It has been dramatically and tragically confirmed. Sconer talked to me quite amicably last Sunday evening and appeared anxious to help my enquiries. On Monday morning, after he had heard from Parker, who alone was in his confidence, that I had seen Mrs. Ricks, he suddenly asked me to throw up the whole case and leave the district.

"Then, last night when I told Parker that I knew of the operation for abortion *and who was responsible for it,* it brought things to a head. I was 'shattering an illusion' of Parker's because he thought no one knew that the man responsible was Sconer, and, a loyal soul, he was dismayed. As Matron told me he 'was in the study with Sconer for half an hour immediately afterwards', and since I had also said that all this would come out at the Inquest, Sconer knew that it was all up with him and decided to commit suicide that night.

"How he did this you know."

Carolus then, briefly and as though making a military report, described how he had heard Sconer pass his door

212

and seen him leave the grounds; how he had followed him to the church and into the tower and how he had attempted to prevent his suicide.

"That it was suicide I think you, Superintendent, know now, unless I am mistaken in my guess that the memorandum handed to you just now was to the effect that a suicide note had been found in the pocket of the dead man."

Osborne said nothing. But Mr. Gorringer felt it was time for one of his—on the whole—welcome interruptions.

"I own myself bewildered by the turn things have taken," he said. "I have known Cosmo Sconer for many years and should never have suspected him of libertinage with a member of his own staff. However, that conceded the rest follows. To rid himself of a blackmailer he was constrained to murder and suicide."

"Suicide," said Carolus. "I haven't suggested that Sconer murdered Sime. But it's time for a drink. What about it, Mr. Pocket?"

Pocket turned to Osborne.

"No objection?" he asked.

The large head moved slowly from side to side in a grudging negative.

"What will it be then?" asked Pocket brightly.

"I scarcely know," said Mr. Gorringer. "What would be an appropriate drink, I wonder. It is 4 a.m. Superintendent?"

The short lips scarcely seemed to move yet the incredible words were enunciated clearly enough.

"A Cherry Brandy."

Carolus stared aghast and as soon as drinks were poured hastened to continue, as though to cover the policeman's eccentricity.

"So Sime was angling away quite happily at one point," he said. "With three lines out and nibbles on two of them.

213

He might have continued till he was proprietor of the school if someone had not decided that things had gone far enough. There was a bold, ingenious and nearly successful plan to make Sime the victim of what would be taken to be a fatal accident. By the merest chance, still difficult to understand, he failed. If he succeeded and Sime had died from a fall from the tower which he had climbed to spy on others, St. Asprey's School would not now be in a jeopardy.

"The plan was this. While Sime was on top of the tower almost any preparations could be made below of which he would remain unaware. The would-be murderer intended to hide behind the curtains near the top of the spiral staircase and as Sime took the first few steps downward impel him violently to perdition. This, as far as he could see, would leave no evidence at all. Bruises on the body would be plentiful and accountable for by the fall downstairs, and there would be no witnesses.

"But this was not enough. A shove on the stairs might be ineffectual for Sime was a powerful and heavy man. What was necessary was something to trip him and the would-be murderer measured the width of the staircase and cut a bough of yew to give him, when it was trimmed, a perfect obstacle which would trip anyone who had not seen it, even if he were not already falling. This he set just round the first bend of the staircase. It was carefully made just too long to go from wall to wall so that it had to be forced into position about a foot above the level of the stairs, and because it was freshly cut it left two green marks on the wall. When I found these, and Skippett told me of the trimmings of the bough he had found in the hedge of the churchyard, I knew for certain that Sime's fall had been no accident, but that someone was determined to kill him.

"It was a miracle that Sime survived that attempt. The

214

loft was more than thirty foot up and the stairs were worn and precipitous. I think it left him more shattered than he admitted or showed. He had to get himself taken back to the school after it, and not to hospital, because only from the school could he conduct his blackmailing activities. With him out of the way, he thought, Sconer and Duckmore would get out of hand and perhaps combine against him. But he was scared enough to sleep with a loaded revolver under his pillow.

"He had good cause to be. Whoever had failed in his attempt on the stairs was determined not to fail again. Once again it would be an 'accident' but this time there would be no doubt of its effect."

"So," interrupted Mr. Gorringer, "we are to take it that the author of the attempt in the tower was also the murderer of Sime?"

"Even on the staff of a preparatory school," said Carolus, "you would scarcely be likely to find two deliberate and plotting murderers at the same time, surely. Of course it was the same person, and a very determined person at that."

"What did I say?" burst out Mrs. Skippett. "I told you, didn't I? It was that Duckmore. I said he had a funny look about him and those eyes seemed to look right through you till they gave you the creeps."

Osborne emitted a short but audible sigh.

"Please finish your statement, Deene," he said.

Carolus decided to ruffle that smug impassivity.

"I first suspected that Jumbo Parker was the murderer..." he began quietly.

But he produced his effect. Osborne sat bolt upright and shouted "*What?*"

"Didn't you hear? I'm sorry. I said I first suspected Parker was the murderer when I learned how he was supposed to have found Sime's body after the fall in the tower. For as Sime told me, he left his car at the gate of the church. Now either he had arrived there and gone up to the top of the tower *before* Parker came to play the organ, or he entered the church *while* Parker was there. In either case Parker was aware of him in the tower. Why should he invent that story of a strange noise behind the tower door and his alarm and horror when Sime, unconscious, rolled out of the tower? Someone could have entered the church before either of them, hidden behind the curtains where the bell-ringers hung their coats and while Sime was on the tower set his obstruction and waited, again behind the curtains, to push him down. He would also have had to get back to the school unseen before Sime was brought back. But who? It would have been necessary for him to go there early in the afternoon and remain there till after Sime had been taken away, risking a possible search of the tower when Sime was found. And who, among those who any sort of a motive for killing Sime, could it have been? Mayring was with the Away team, Duckmore, Stanley, Kneller, the Ferrises and Mollie all on the archery lawn at different times that afternoon and Sconer interviewing parents at the school.

"But I only say I suspected Parker. Horlick and Skippett, if one could conceive of either as a murderer, were unaccounted for and there was always the possibility of an enemy of Sime of whom we know nothing. . ."

"Did you say Skippett?" asked Mrs. Skippett. "My husband. . ."

"Yes, I know," said Carolus quickly and soothingly. "Nobody ever suspected him. There was however the question of motive and this for a time defeated me until I saw more of Parker and realized his extraordinary obsession with the school and his pathetic loyalty to Sconer. I liked Parker and realized the pathos of his wasted life—

twenty years given to building up that school from eight boys, as he told me, to its recent success. He could not conceive of any future except at St. Asprey's and he knew Sime was blackmailing Sconer. He saw his life falling apart unless Sime could be eliminated by an 'accident'. He had the simplicity in some things of a child, and a child's cunning, too. Sconer extolled his loyalty and devotion and Parker made no secret of it.

"So having failed in his first attempt he made plans for a second. This time there was to be no doubt. It was again to look like an accident and it shows some of Parker's simplicity that he really believed Sime's death would be taken as an archery mishap.

"What he intended to do was to drug Sime after lunch and during the afternoon *stab him with the head of a broadhead arrow* afterwards screwing in the shaft to make it appear that Sime had been shot by accident from the lawn.

"He had everything planned. He had stolen a small supply of Mollie Westerly's very small quick-acting sleeping pills and after lunch went to Matron's room and was seen by her at the medicine cupboard. Matron thought he was helping himself to an aspirin as he often did for a hang-over but in fact he was taking one of Fitzsmith's capsules which could be opened to allow him to insert five or six of Mollie's sleeping pills. Matron afterwards discovered that one was missing.

With this prepared he went down to Sime's room and Mrs. Skippett noticed him passing through the hall. He had Sime's confidence—as Mayring said, he and Parker were the only two who spoke to Sime. As a matter of fact Parker inspired everyone's confidence—Sally O'Maverick used to call him 'Uncle Jumbo'—and he would have no difficulty in persuading Sime to swallow the capsule on some pretext or other. He then left Sime, propped up on his pillows, to fall

217

into a heavy drugged sleep, and returned to his room, again passing Mrs. Skippett in the hall."

"Well, if I'd of known!" exclaimed Mrs. Skippett. "Whoever was to think of such a thing? No one wouldn't have dreamed it, not in a thousand years. And you mean to say. . ."

"He stayed in his room for a full hour during which he deliberately poured away two inches from his bottle of whisky. He knew that Matron would observe this and report that he had been boozing all the afternoon. He had his weapon ready, for on the previous afternoon he had gone to the summer-house where Kneller kept his arrows and extracted a broadhead arrow. He had done this while the archers were walking down towards their targets for the summer-house was kept locked except during practice. He had pushed it down the leg of his trousers which caused him to walk in a peculiarly stiff-legged way and when I met him on his way in he had to explain this as 'rheumatism'. It was noticeable that when I asked him about his rheumatism that evening he could scarcely think for a moment what I meant. He now unscrewed the arrow, put the head with its few inches of shaft in his pocket and the shaft itself (shorter by the head than when he had brought it from the summer-house) inside his jacket. I would guess that he cut a hole in the bottom of the inside breast pocket of his jacket and pushed most of the shaft through so that he could draw it out in a moment but could walk quite naturally.

"I think it was at the last minute that he thought of fingerprints and realized that he would need gloves. He had none of his own for it was the summer term but he had become, in those years, enough a member of the family to know where Sconer kept his. He went very silently—so silently that even Matron's trained ears did not hear him—to the Sconer's room and took the gloves he needed.

"Towards three o'clock he came out of his room again to go by the way through from the private part of the house on the first floor to the boy's dormitories and so down to the staff bungalow. This time Matron caught the sound of his footsteps but just at that moment her attention was held by the sight of the two boys escaping from the cricket field to go to Sime's window. This was something she could not miss and she let the footsteps go.

"Parker made his way down. He had drawn Sime's curtains before he left him and found him now in the half darkened room in deep sleep. He stabbed him with a single blow severing the jugular vein, leaving the arrowhead deep in the wound. He screwed in the shaft of the arrow and then, according to plan crossed to open the curtains—for it was to be a stray arrow from outside that had killed Sime. The two boys had meanwhile approached, seen the curtain drawn, and in their own words 'scooted back to the cricket field'. Parker looked cautiously out, I imagine, saw no one in the vicinity, drew back the curtains and returned to his room."

"An excellent account of things," said Mr. Gorringer. "But I for one remain unconvinced. I daresay you are right in saying that Sime was stabbed, but I cannot see that you have more than circumstantial evidence against Parker. Why could not some other hand have done what you say he did?"

"Whoever killed him by stabbing screwed on the shaft of the arrow afterwards," said Carolus. "This can *only* mean that he intended it to look as though Sime had been shot. He would therefore in his actions that afternoon have avoided, at all costs, being on the archery lawn or in any place from which an arrow could have been shot through Sime's window. Parker was the only person in, or connected with the school who did that. It was evident from the first

219

that Sime was stabbed and not shot. No marksman in the world could shoot a man *inside a room* through the adam's apple with a single shot at forty-five yards. William Tell couldn't have done it. No one among the archers could even be sure of hitting the innermost ring of the target with his first arrow and on the range the target was standing at a fixed distance in a clear light. You play darts? Try throwing from a slightly different distance, nearer to or farther from the target, and you lose all control. To suggest that any archer could turn round from the archery lawn and calmly shoot an arrow into a man's throat at *any* distance is absurd, and when the man is lying inside a room it becomes preposterous. That should have been obvious from the very first to anyone knowing the details. So the people on the archery lawn that afternoon, so far from being suspects, were the very ones who were free from all suspicion. And that left only Parker.

"But when you say the evidence—at least for a trial on a charge of murder—is circumstantial, I agree. I must point out that the police and not I have the means of supporting it with more tangible evidence. There is, for instance, the age-old matter of bloodstains. It would have been impossible to do what Parker did without getting blood on his clothes—at least on his sleeve—and I noticed that on that evening he broke all precedents by changing for dinner. Now a blood-stained coat is not an easy thing to get rid of and has provided essential evidence before now. There are several other points which will already have occurred to the Detective Superintendent here. Like the gloves. I can only say what I believe—no, what I *know*—happened. I leave it to the police to prove it to the satisfaction of a jury."

"What about Duckmore and his confession?"

"The only thing I *know* about Duckmore is that he did not kill Sime. He is so full of the illusions of guilt, poor chap, that it is impossible to sort out the facts from his various stories. I think it possible that he did shoot an arrow at Sime's window, and it may even have broken the glass of the picture above Sime's head. If so he recovered the arrow when he went into Sime's room (as he did) before Mayring discovered the body. But even about that I am uncertain. He could have broken the glass himself, but Horlick did find an arrow in the rose-garden on the other side of the house, and Duckmore might have thrown it away. We may know more about that when the case against Parker has been proved. As a matter of fact, in view of Sconer's suicide and the end of hope for the school as at present constituted, I should not be surprised if Parker confessed."

Osborne, very quietly but distinctly, made his only relevant observation.

"He has," he said and closing his notebook with a snap walked out of the room.